Dancing the Maze

Kenneth Dawson

Dancing the Maze

PretendGeniusPress

London, New York, San Francisco, Seattle, Washington D.C.

PretendGeniusPress
www.pretendgenius.com

ISBN: 0-9747261-9-2

Printed in the United States of America

CONTENTS

Paralysis

I. Country Life

1

We lived the life new-wavers dream of in a log cabin on bottomland in a hollow between wooded hills. We had no electricity or inside plumbing and went to a shack out back to shit.

Was nearly bitten by a copperhead there, at age four, sat down beside it and when my step grandfather saw and told me to sit still I jumped instead. The strike somehow missed and Chet beat it flat with a piece of pipe using up on the snake his anger at my being so silly.

Fell there into a ditch full of cut briars piled for burning and carry the scars still. There were ticks in the yard and they would hold me down screaming and burn them off with cigarettes.

We had a fat old sow I used to ride – the family had pictures. She dropped a litter every year and promptly crushed them. No malice or intent, just careless obesity and flat-smashed, innards-busted, dead, baby pigs. Every year the same damned thing and the buzzards formed a lunch line in the trees.

I remember it as a cold, hard time when you didn't raise anything you couldn't eventually kill and eat and most people worked till they ached just for their three a day.

Men were polite to each other; umbrage could cause blood to flow and everyone I knew was trying to get the hell out of the new-wavers' dream, at least to someplace where you could shit indoors and have one of those magic levers that, when pushed, causes clear, clean water to flow.

A north central Arkansas tarpaper shack with the back porch well and water bucket and the pig butchered on the kitchen table. My father's leatherwork to stretch the pension dole and the boxer dog and the backyard boulders.

The cramped bunk beds whose twins I met years later aboard ship.

Grandpa George killing the snake at the back steps with a hatchet and the others that died to my mother's hoe and the black one I ran into sprinting around the back corner, but was gone before I returned with a good stick and there were a lot of damned snakes.

The old man across the road who still plowed his garden with a mule and the old, old woman called Little Mary who lived in what used to be a store always telling how her gallstones flew about the surgical theater when they made the incision?

Great grandmother in another of her little white houses still chopping her own wood and hiding those damned new pennies I spent half my childhood looking for (she was a Jewess and a poet and they said I got it from her).

Mother trying to give me drawing lessons from mail-order John Gnagy kits because somebody told her I had talent and Boyer's Garage that was a smithy before and the school with two classes in each room and wood stoves so we all had to go fetch wood and got and extra short recess. That old bitch Brady who thought some of my drawings were obscene and disliked me the whole year, the only teacher who ever spanked me besides a rapped knuckle or two.

The hills and red clay ditches and just rocky Arkansas where we children hunted each other in a thousand variations on a theme and shot each other with BB guns having been told so often that someone would get an eye shot out that we figured it was destiny so why worry about it?

Coming back at night from a chili supper at the school my mother carrying a piece of pie for my father when she fell on the difficulty, rocky, downhill path and fell hard but saved my father's pie and another night returning from something else when I fell down a ditch-hole and Grandma Moore jumped in after me.

A rotted out tool shed in back where I fought a child's war with the wasps trying to shoot their nests down with a bow and arrow and getting properly stung and stumbling across a yellow jacket nest in the grass and escaping unstung and the scorpion my bare-footed mother stepped on that should have stung her but didn't.

A sickly old pear tree I was told not to climb so made a special effort to do so whenever possible by the outhouse where I feared the spiders and falling in and why are there always bees buzzing in a summer outhouse?

Sleeping on the living room sofa in winter with my brother because the stove wouldn't heat our back porch closet-bedroom with the bunks and even then a bookshelf because they insisted on fostering my interest so that I owned books before I started school and then belonged to a club that sent me Oliver Twist and stories about Daniel Boone (I read that Natty Bumpo really couldn't shoot the heads off of flying tomahawks with a Kentucky rifle but refused to believe knowing that in a year or two when I got my .22 I'd be doing the same thing).

The fence-line outcroppings that were perfect for warring and damsel-saving and bear-fighting where savage pantomimes were carried out with the real knives, hatchets, screwdrivers and chisels that were my playthings and never hurting myself. Falling off of the outcroppings, off of the shed, out of trees, down the hills, into the ditches and never hurting myself.

II: Paralysis

My father was at the point of death for a couple years.
He lay in bed looking out through glaring eyes
that gave no evidence of seeing anything.

Curious that the most influential event of my life was a disease and this not mine, but an affliction of my father's.

When he was twenty-eight, when I was three and my brother eight, in 1954 my father snuffled a microbe and never walked again.

A polio bug. He had the symptoms of a common cold for about a week, then one morning tried to get out of bed and discovered that his legs wouldn't work.

Infantile paralysis. The Salk vaccine had been developed, but hadn't hit the streets yet. Indeed my brother and I, high-risk exposees, were inoculated out of the first units to reach the Midwest.

It was still experimental.

My father died and was revived. He spent six months in an iron lung when his own lungs wouldn't work. He had a machine to help him cough when he couldn't. His arms and legs withered, his fingers stiffened and curled, his diaphragm collapsed. One hospital got him past the threat of death and sent him on to another for rehabilitation. He was in hospital for two years.

My brother and I saw him rarely; we were too young. When he went away for therapy my mother went with him and we children checked in at our grandparent's house, the first move of childhoods spent in other people's homes.

> I've witnessed men and animals there before, as death curled about them, dreadfully injured and lying quietly, but I can't say if they were at peace or wrapped in flaming agony without the strength to scream.

My father, a bitter shade in his wheelchair, went through his hell of being nearly killed and crippled and could not resist giving hell to us. Not in huge, hysterical splurges, but by bits.

Small daily doses.

He couldn't beat us, but his tongue was a flensing knife and he flayed us, pared us down until we no longer cast a shadow.

It wasn't all bitterness. My father was trying to teach us the truth about life, a courageous experiment this.

Having been so severely trashed himself, he was trying to ready his children by raising them without the myth of happiness. His teaching included object lessons.

I was ten and my brother fifteen. My father had a carport built behind the house. This was a wooden carport and it needed staining. Dad hired my brother and I offering what seemed a fortune at the time.

Probably twenty bucks or so.

We stained it and when we were done Dad told us we hadn't done a good enough job and refused to pay us.

Not one penny.

That's life.

Dad's personal holocaust taught him some truth about life that dismayed him. His reaction was to give up on life and put his money on heaven. And to quit telling his sons those nice lies adults tell children, all that business about dreams and success and fulfillment. He made our childhood rough because he didn't want us to get the wrong idea.

An admirable idea, but it worked too well. My brother and I learned failure so well that we gave up on trying to do anything much. My brother works in restaurants washing dishes and busing tables. A nice line of work if you're not interested in making much money. When a boss or co-worker gives my brother a taste of that hell humans are so happy to dispense, he just leaves.

There's always another restaurant.

You must intuit my brother. He never speaks unless you get him into a corner and poke him until he squeaks. You practically have to point a gun at him, demand speech or his life, then he looks at the floor and lets the words drop out, awkward and apprehensive in the harsh light.

> The last two years of my father's life doctors suggested that I let him die. He was on a ventilator and the considered opinion was that he wouldn't survive long if taken off of it. And this is what the doctors thought I should do. Not that they actually said it. They hinted, heavily. 'Quality of life' was mentioned often, this being the measure by which we decide what life we preserve and what life we allow to flicker out, if we don't actually extinguish it. Think about his 'quality of life' they said. Brother, did I ever. I wonder if they did. Dad, himself, wasn't talking. When awake, he only stared.

After we brought him home from the he'd tune in weathermen on the radio, but didn't hear them. He was listening to the wind, wary of its faltering, the dead calm that precedes cyclones.

He'd just been born in the Veterans' Hospital in Memphis, Tennessee. It was the second time.

By then his lungs were working well enough that he didn't have to live in an iron lung. By then his strength was back enough that he didn't always have pneumonia. By then he was beginning to live this life he hadn't expected. The life of a near quadriplegic, no longer bipedal with wizened, weakened arms and stiffened crooks for fingers; a life in which he couldn't go to bed or get dressed or sit on the toilet without help. A life traveled in a wheelchair.

Part of his birth was a tornado. It hit a town and hurt so many people the regular hospitals ran out of room and the VA took some in. As part of his birth he saw these victims brought in to live or die, people hurt in strange and obscene ways. Part of his birth was to discover a terror he'd not found before, not even on Omaha Beach.

When he came home we all lived under the reign of his terror. He monitored the radio and the skies and believed in foreshadowing. The first cloud's blunt nose, a darkening on the horizon sent us to a neighbor who had a storm cellar and he'd round up another neighbor or two and they would thump-thump-thump ease him down the steps into the underground where we, my mother, brother and I sat with them, Dad and his fear, waiting.

Sometimes we'd be alone and sometimes the shelter would be packed and my father sat with his terror, hardly room for the two of them in his chair, waiting for the wind to die.

> I wasn't ready to make a judgment. I had no idea what the quality of his life was, but it was the only life he had. I refused to decide for him if it was worth living and, finally, he made the move himself passing away in spite of his mechanical supports.

He was, I assume, ready for the end when it arrived.

Dad had been waiting for a long time. He was tired of his wheelchair. He wanted to walk the streets of glory.

He liked to have things tied up and had prearranged his cremation. By the time I got there to bury him he was incinerated and packaged leaving behind only a minor dishevelment of Bible courses, Glenn Miller albums and old clothes.

In his room I sat in his wheelchair: they're very comfortable if you sit with the knowledge that you can get up again. There were plenty of Christian writings to read. Dad had been in training for death for years, ever since the polio. With translations and concordances and histories he sought the true word, researched his way to God. Studied his deity as others investigate cells using scholarship as his road to salvation.

No comparative religious texts; nothing on Zen or Islam or Zoroaster. He put his money on Christ and never looked back.

He didn't dare.

You're supposed to feel something when your father dies, when you stand to as they dig the hole and inter the discarded shell, but I did not.

Our relationship with its stunning variations on bitterness and compassion had eventually ended with nothing. The roller coaster burned all my emotional fuel.

There was no funeral in the traditional sense. Partly because that's what he wanted and I still, after all those years, felt an obligation to do as he wished. But I also knew I didn't have it in me to fake my way through a 'normal' funeral with the sympathies and grief. I did dress for the occasion with a jacket and tie a small group – mother, my brother and wife and I gathered at the cemetery.

A fellow in a plaid jacket and jeans brought what had once been a man in a little plastic box, drove it from the funeral home in a Chevy panel truck. He dug the hole there by grandma's grave, dug it like he was putting in a shrub, a couple of measured feet deep, put Dad's cremains, the burnt offering, in and covered it up. Then he shook hands all around and left.

III: Tactical Reasons

The dragon is of such immensity that human vision, even that of gifted men, seers and scholars, can encompass only bits of the beast, must imagine its presence and in dreams alone can its totality be suspected.

In Vientiene there was a whorehouse called Madam Lulu's. It was run by an old French woman and you couldn't get laid there. The only service offered was fellatio. It was a marvelous place: a girl could have a career as a prostitute at Madame Lulu's and retire a virgin.

One of the girls taught me to chase the dragon. Her bar name was Aron, her real name a secret she would tell the man she loved, if he thought to ask her.

Aron cooked number two heroin over a spirits burner and inhaled the fumes through a beaten silver tube decorated with demonic monkeys in bas-relief; ape devils from the Ramakien. Say Asia to me and I think of Aron sucking dreams through her monkey-chased tube.

I still had this habit when I was advising a unit of Royal Thai Border Patrol Police. I was supposed to be teaching them intelligence gathering techniques. One hundred meters down the road across the border in the Kingdom of Laos was a Kuomontang base that was actually a refinery, opium into heroin. They too had an American advisor, a spec five named Reed.

The KMT paid the Thai general in command of the district a percentage and the real purpose of the Border Patrol station was to make sure the cut was straight.

We had a phone line run in between us and Reed called every day. He was always hungry to talk to another Westerner. By then I found most Americans boring. Their world view was so simplistic, everything in straight lines and I considered Reed's calls a burden, like being polite to an idiot relative. He called the day before his death and said, "They're holding out."

"I know."

"The chinks won't pay."

"Get fucked," I said.

I had taken to telling Reed to get fucked automatically when he used words like chink or gook or slope, which he did a lot. He ignored it thinking it just one more example of my weirdness. I considered him, a man with a Kowloon Chinese wife who still said gook, insane.

"They're mounting up here."

I said nothing, find it difficult to talk to people who use phrases like 'mounting up.'

"Think it'll get down to shooting?"

"Probably some, part of the bargaining process."

"What you going to do?"

"I'll be with my people," I said.

"Are you straight?" Reed asked.

"Relatively," I said.

The shooting began that night and ended about dawn. I took four men out in a looping flanking movement and there was a lot of noise and nonsense, some actual contact, much shadow shooting. Reed was killed somewhere in there. Two days later when a new deal had been cut and we were anti-communist allies again I went over to bring Reed's body back to Thailand and ship him home, another martyr of the holy war.

2

I used to dig deep pits with short shovels in which I would stand to in that strange chalky darkness just before dawn and stare into the trees trying to pick out a shape that hadn't been there before, a shape that needed killing.

And we dug a smaller, deeper hole at one end of the pit's floor. This was for grenades. When a grenade came into the pit you were supposed to kick it into the deeper hole and curl yourself into the opposite side of the pit covering your head, bringing your knees up into the good old fetal position to wait out the blast.

The good old fetal position was SOP.

3

I had to join some people in the field, had to do it by parachute and I'd not had jump training.

They gave me a day. I went to a little airstrip where a guy in cut-off fatigue pants and a t-shirt told me about capewells and streamers and tree landings. He made me jump off an oil drum to practice the roll and showed me how to exit out the side door of a little, gray, Cessna with no markings.

We went to lunch and that afternoon I made my first jump, a static line. I had a dummy ripcord, was supposed to pull it and show the jumpmaster I knew how. I had to go freefall as there was the possibility of people shooting at me on the way down. The idea was to fall as far as possible before opening the canopy.

On the ground jumpmaster said "Okay," and gave me another chute and I went up for my first free fall. It was my last jump. The next morning someone had changed their mind and I went somewhere else to do something altogether different.

4

By then I understood that it didn't matter much to the people on the ground who came into the village, us or the enemy. In any case they were shit out of luck.

I did notice some variations in the atrocities suffered. They, for example, didn't rape as much as we did. Or burn and destroy property, but they did tend toward the more symbolic such as cutting out the tongues of those who spoke for the government. Our mutilations were done to the dead, a matter of trophies.

Both sides tortured when it seemed the thing to do. The group I was with considered itself above such things. We never raped except as an occasional, individual aberration. We did mutilate the dead, remove heads and genitalia and so on, but this was psychological warfare and was done to dead soldiers. We had little to do with villagers. We did torture, not out of meanness or boredom, but only when we needed information. We always had tactical reasons.

Later, in another country, there was a bounty paid on enemy heads, a considerable sum for the local troopers and I once packed a basket of heads for a fifteen year old who'd taken so many he couldn't carry them all.

He was too happy to contain himself, grinning and dancing down the trail. His family was in a camp. The head money would do wonders for them.

5

What I heard mostly was the roar of blood in my ears, a saline rush.

In action the problem is confusion. Nothing goes the way it's planned, you spend your time dealing with surprises and fuck-ups and you reach a point when you simply can't see or hear any more.

I used to check out, become a droid going through the motions, doing what I was supposed to, even though my personality, my identity, my emotions had gone south. The overall situation was of no importance. I dealt with what came before me.

Once I saw my wrist break open and blood come out. The droid decided that, as the blood wasn't spurting and the hand still functioned, it was unimportant and dismissed it with less exasperation than I would feel over a flat tire today.

I was in this state when I first actually saw someone go down by my hand. Usually we received fire from foliage whereupon we would fire into the foliage until the incoming fire stopped. This time I was there and he was there and he dropped.

I suppose it was some aspect of the droid state that drove me to go over and examine the corpse I'd created.

A boy, young even to me, and I was a child. I opened the shirt carefully rather than ripping it. We were strangely gentle with the dead though we gave the living hell. It was necessary for me to see where I had violated the body's integrity; let the air in, the vitality out.

I was regarding the holes when taken by an unusual quality of the chest; a certain fleshiness about the upper ribs and the droid informed me that if I sat this boy up this fleshiness would stand out to become breasts and this wasn't a boy at all.

6

You came upon it sometimes, stumbled over it without warning.

He had landed against a tree trunk and was sitting there watching our approach. His leg, attached by skin and muscle, was twisted up beside him so that his sandaled foot was touching his ear. His other leg was down the path.

We all stepped over it.

A middle-aged man with some gray in his mustashe. As we neared, he closed his eyes.

"I'll get it," one of us said pulling a Siamese bush knife, more like a long-handled cleaver, from a basketry sheath at his back and the rest of us moved on.

He caught up and later we learned the bush knife wasn't used. He'd put it away, got out his morphine (we all carried lots of morphine) and put the man to sleep.

7

I was sitting in the radio shack with the talker when I heard the mortar round hit, heard one out by the perimeter and then I was blown through the wall and into the side of the bunker next door.

You'll have to consult Hemingway to read about being in the center of an explosion. Look in *A*

Farewell To Arms, page 54 of the Scribner's edition. I don't remember, haven't the slightest idea.

I do remember a notion of suspension, of being neither here or there and impact and falling to another impact. No pain to speak of, but a humming vibration over my skin like the play of static electricity, St. Elmo's Fire. And an inflation that rose from my belly up through my chest and rattled out past my lips. And the sound in my head, a sort of whistled whine – not one but a keening chorus.

Quite a fight I was later told. Parts of the camp were overrun, lots of screaming and death, that sort of thing. I remember a couple of running men stumbling over my body. They paid me no mind. A vague thought that I should move, at least get out of people's way, but I couldn't. My dazed and perplexed body was as futile as a jellyfish on the shore.

Not that it worried me. I had no worries.

I was loopy. A projectile of some sort – shrapnel or a piece of the radio shack or a piece of the radio talker – had collided with my skull at that point where my forehead bends back to provide a roof for my brain. It removed some skin and hair, left a modest hole and knocked me loony.

I lay there and looked up. The night was full of lights; lights that sparked and lights that screamed, lights that billowed and grew, lights that sprang to life and drifted slowly down and arcing, staccato lights, red and yellow, that sped across my vision and died in flight.

8

That lieutenant wasn't too bad, but he got himself killed making a career move.

An Army career is much helped by citations for valor in your file. To be cited, an officer must be recommended by two other officers who observed this valor. Officers stuck in the rear would, in the evenings and on weekends, talk their way into a quarter-ton, find out where the nearest action was and drive that way until they heard gunfire.

This was one of the game's rules. You had to be able to hear gunfire. When they heard shooting they would cite each other and go home.

But the lieutenant and his two friends took a wrong turn and got too close to the action. Perhaps it was over-enthusiasm.

They all got iced by some raggedy-assed guerillas with no careers to speak of.

9

When I went AWOL...I don't know. I think it was because of the kids.

I had a thing for the kids, they broke my heart. I guess I was just weird. Guys would talk, you know, about the little girl. Charlie would talk the little girl into carrying a bomb up to the big soldiers and exploding it. Would blow up the soldiers and the little girl and the guys used to say what a terrible thing it was to do to the soldiers. I used to think what a terrible thing it was to do to a little girl.

I had an attitude problem.

My room was in a converted go-down. It was like a longhouse, open to the ends, dark inside as the forest. The center of the building was open and dirt-floored. The rooms-for-rent, more closed-off stalls, built of planking against the walls. There was a communal water supply where you washed with water dipped with aluminum bowls, and two propane tanks with burners for cooking. Bargirls lived there and shop girls and factory workers and a couple-three women who cared for the bargirls' children; lots of children half Thai and half Anglo or black or Mexican.

Mornings I would fill a teapot with Polaris water and go down to the burners to heat it for Nescafe. I wore a t-shirt and wrap and flip flops and would squat waiting for the water to boil. The children stopped their play and came to witness me, the pale thing among them. I'd stopped shaving and they had never seen a bearded man.

Later I put on pants and went to the market for beer and cigarettes, liter bottles of Singh, short packets of Gold Citys. In the room I smoked and drank and practiced thinking about nothing. The door would be open for the breeze and the children would stand there watching the hair grow on the farang's face and dreaming of their fathers.

10

The captain of intelligence was afraid of me, thought I was probably instinctively homicidal.

I wound down somewhat earlier than the rest, decided not to play anymore.

The rifle belt with its paraphernalia of death made my back ache. The helmet hurt my head. I decided not to bear them any longer.

They gave me a sugar billet when I came back from deserting. They knew what was going on, but didn't know what to do about it; send me to the doctor or prison or what so they made me this captain of intelligence's driver, easy duty, and hoped it would go away. Not that they were concerned about me, it was the medals they wore that demanded deference.

And I knew secrets. If you're not will to shoot them, you must be careful with people who know secrets.

So when I stopped the quarter-ton so the captain of intelligence could go confer with a contact, when I was supposed to dismount and take up a defensive position by the road, when I didn't, but kept my seat and smoked a cigarette while waiting, the captain didn't say a word.

The Blues You Play

Scent Hounds

The scent of us dogs trail is ourselves:
bits we shed from womb to grave; flakes of skin,
splinters of speech, contrails of thought,
a comet's tail of sparking
shredded ice through the void
we broadcast ourselves along our paths;
twisting and crossing, combining with ground
rock and diesel fumes to make each other sneeze.

Pets

The trouble with wild things is memory.

At that little café outside Chang Rai
the gibbon,
on a tether from the rafters was for a long time good,
capering, sweetly stealing food from plates,
goosing the waitresses
until the day he remembered,
felt the chain
and bit off half a German woman's face.

Drive

Did you ever drive at night
faster than your lights,
foot down and dims on so that by the time
something is seen,

you're already past it?
Racing on the long slab, just right of the yellow,
able to dream, for a bit,
that by going far enough fast enough
you can leave all you've broken behind
and get ahead to all that nothing?

Sacrifice

He was a big, red rooster
loud and cocky like a rooster should be.
Stay away from him my grandma said,
Grandpa too. "He'll get you."
Children being what they are I
was attracted to that rooster without recourse,
stalked him, pushed him,
edged closer and closer until, finally,
he got me.
I carry the scars still.
I thought they'd be mad at me but it was the
rooster that lost his head and showed up stewed,
the next Sunday.

Firecracker

He held the hand out before him
delicately,
balanced at the end of his wrist
blooded
bones snapped and thrusting from the ruptured flesh
Like something
fragile he wanted badly to set down
somewhere safe while Don, who had brought
the fireworks,
stood fixed,

his staring eyes more open than they had ever been,
saying,
Jesus Christ, Jesus Christ, Jesus Christ.

Alms

Soul's scars bind his gait,
a limping shuffle and he squats,
with the truth as he knows it. Declares it,
"spare change?"

The Blues You Play

The blues you play, walking through one day's
geography, waking to lunching to nodding; mapping
the night until the next, new licks from step to step;

But turn around and the theme has changed, the half-
finished riff irrelevant.

Parenting

The child you failed loves you still. Why? Why? As
the new one, a bright sound fumbling at your knees,
this anticipated failure scarring you already. A dog
left you once because you couldn't love - a dog - so
you expect nothing of women and children, only their
wising up, giving up, but he returns, over and over,
saying 'Hi Dad,' and you are humbled.

Millennium

On that road in Iowa a flock of sparrows became a dragon, twisting upon itself and up, beyond sanity, into the new year's sky, leaving me simple and heavy on the pavement.

Camus saw it as did Eisenly and Steinbeck, the dragon's secret always evident and everywhere: the plains and forests and reefs.

Sharks dart at minnows, find a great serpent they can nibble, but whose heart is inviolate.

Terrible and heartening, I wanted, at once, to flee and pursue.

The Bigot

The dream he dreamed grew legs and staggers, limping and lumpen, through the world leaving a bad taste, foul odor in the minds of all who trip over it.

It, this dream, makes no sense, is lunacy but he dreamed it and it won't die, can't be killed as long as he dreams it with love and desperation over all our cries.

The world protests – he turns his back and dreams it still.

Human Condition

There was a Nazi who saved Chinese in Nanking and a Japanese who saved Jews in Europe.

Hold tight, hold tight.

There was a Nazi who saved Chinese in Nanking and a Japanese who saved Jews in Europe.

At least I have someone to pray to.

Hold tight. Hold tight.

Ghosts

So I bought the place and started to live in the old house, but there were too many ghosts. In the parlor, kitchen and every bedroom the ghosts stood shoulder to shoulder.

There was a ghost on the crapper in the bathroom, a ghost gave me the finger from the hallway mirror, a ghost dog growled from the parlor rug.

Finally I said goddammit and left the house to them. They smirked to each other as I walked out the door. I live in a cabin farther back on the property: the house and barn are between it and the road. There's a ghost in the cabin too, but it's a little one and I can handle it.

Darkness and Light

Despite the law, in 1968, the dark people still kept to the balcony leaving the corners for pale lovers so that when they stopped the movie the evening following that afternoon in Memphis, announced he was dead, the light people, a theater full of them, were cheering and the dark people, silent, looking down.

Water Rights

The rich had plumbing, the poor had wells, the wretched only cisterns and the rain's mercy.

Our well was a ceramic pipe thrust up through the back porch floor, going down to the sweet water hole with an aluminum dipper contraption that caught water like mice in a trap.

I was proud of it. The really poor had to go outside.

Vision

I knew a man once who'd spoken to God, or rather listened as God spoke to him. He dared no reply.

I knew a man once who'd spoken to God, or rather listened as God spoke to him. He dared no reply.

GODSPOKETOHIM on an uphill stretch of Arkansas Highway 62 where it comes into Batesville.

I knew a man once who'd spoken to God.

The Wilderness Revisited

Last Saturday week at the county rummage sale around the Confederate monument on the courthouse lawn I bought, second or third hand, a sweat-stained, gray wool afternoon in a copper-headed wood of ankle-twisting stones and oak trees stumbling into blackberry briars to meet a wedge-bottomed minie ball with blood and butternut.

Charles

In pain so deep it's no longer felt my brother slips heedlessly through life untouched, beyond reach, bearing no grudges, slight smile.

The best of scholars he's taken no instruction. Life and circumstance taught him: he transcended by not striving.

Could I I would raise a temple in his name for him to sit and tell nothing.

NBC Warfare

It was waiting in the hard light of 1951 to staple itself firmly to my brain jelly and all the hours of the day finger lightly the back of my mind.

It crowded my morning adventures like a dry-wombed aunt, gave me acne, woke me in hoteled traffic-hummed midnights sweating sloe gin and nicotine.

I trained in an empty hanger to stab ampules into my thigh and wear charcoal cylinders. I traveled smoke-filled chambers with OBA and terror and can tell what's killing me by watching my neighbors.

It travels with me clattering like jade girdle pendants through a generation astride détente that watches walleyed when Conalrad screeches from the monkeyhouse dropping me to my knees with my hands over my eyes.

Love Poem

It seems to fall away at my touch as a child kills butterflies with his clumsy caress.
I feel like a man who has just learned to swim as the last sea dries up, baring the slime to rot in the sun.

Miscarriage

Did you dream child?
Was there time?
Did you in your silent way know life, love it?
Grasp it and strive in the darkness
when the stalking cold stroked your never seen skin,
leeched into the bone?
Did you fight, moan a pre-articulate no?
Did you dream?
Child?
Was there time?

Lichgate Welcome

I dared not witness the wound further wounded so
you clenched came, shivering, to the beginning of
your end, keening the masked chorus behind my
grieving back.

Washed you were and wrapped in your old home's
ruin when I first braved your startled gaze, my soul
hallooing and cringing at once, singing your present
and weeping the inevitable.

Neanderthal Man Faces The Great Cat

He looked, saw, and turned away
to find a stump and make himself part of it,
waiting for his blood to tell him,
gulping air to swell himself and seem more fierce
until the moon's orbit
and a subtle shifting of novas jerked him,
clattering and frightened to courage,
in a surging attack
leaping forward in the people's eye
roaring and hurling darts in the donga.

Siblings

Ground under the same wheel we survived a knotted
Siamese growth, learned in like mires to keep our
peace, walk upright, persisting in life for no good
reason, our common facades serving like carnival
tents to shield the freakish interiors.

We both refuse admission though I, compulsively, lift
the flap, offer a peek.

Coffee Shop

That waitress stepped down off of a slab somewhere
and walked here on legs like white stockings to haunt
the coffee urn her lips painted to life fool no one she
creaks on waterless knees soaking up energy until
sitting, finger jammed into eyeball, staring takes all
my juice and I drink it black.

Stirring is too much trouble.

The Song

Immediately upon finding it, the song, the impulse is
to stifle, be done with that dread rhyme jangling
about the bones.

My skull wishes to be rid of vibrations. Knowledge
without enlightenment, the sense-making bring
serenity is a medicine cabinet razor, a deadly
suggestion.

Intellectualizing is only possible for some, a lie others
can only theorize by day. Night brings honesty that
bruises the soul.

Natural History

In our unknown neighbor's field beyond the gully
where we buried the stillborn calf I found the
coyote's lie of sparrow bones and belly fur in snow
and Johnson stubble and walked backwards through
his day, dancing the grouse tree and hooting down the
rabbit hole: sniffing the coon-fingered creek bank.

On The Death of a Somali Poacher

That fellow, he had too many children perhaps but he loved them on his knee and playing in his little yard. Their cries make his soul sing.

Feeding them was hard, his scant hectares seared and rock-filled, water scarce and his herd underfed. The lion then taking his best cow, the one of fine calves he'd hoped so much for so he dug up the old .303 and two shells and made snares and borrowed a bow with the death painted arrows and crossed over intending to make meat for his children and, with more luck than he ever expected perhaps a tusk or horn that would feed his for longer than he had the arrogance to plan but was shot down quickly by a rhino's bodyguard so that the buses of rich people would have reason to come this way.

Love Poem II

Looking up from my BLT at the Pueblo, Colorado bus station lunch counter I saw her and was ready to give her father my cut-ear buffalo pony, a medicine hat stallion plus two Yellowboy Winchesters and a case of .44 Henry Flats.

On Evolution

Deer twisted by the road.

Since they had toes, accruing like layers of dust forming a stone, a sedimentary process of experience compressed by time into the genes. Solid, inflexible, inexorable. Change so gradual stars die before a decision is made.

No match for the industrial age, accretions that frustrate leopards falter in the headlights, instinct fails. Signals stutter.

Deer twisted by the road.

Sight

Seeing is a practiced art learned through trial and error. A direct gaze is often misleading.

Years ago, standing lookout on the Bering Sea, I learned to detect that on the horizon by looking above it, and trusting to peripherals.

Poetic License

I often wish I'd never heard of whatever it is so that life would calm, newspapers not bother. I spend so much time looking for whatever it is in saloons and temples, Hono and Orlando, Kodiak and Ensenada; can't remember when I first or when I didn't but sometime I almost found it behind my father's chair or under a cowpie.

Went to sea for it jumped out of an airplane after it made love thinking about whatever it is.

Coursed my hip pockets across the dateline below the equator into the Tetons prospecting whatever it is with violence and zazin, discipline and riot and anything short of the needle and gave finally and

forever up on whatever it is as I find it giggling in a
tin cup above a Mobil station's men's room urinal
and backtrack trying to get rid of whatever it is.

Loup Garou

When the full moon squats fat and yellow over the
mountain I feel its fingers tugging at my veins and
with tigerish eyes go away from man and his opinions
into the crazy woods where belligerent deer, dull and
giddy with courage, rattle their antlered pates and
attack my bearish shadow with squirrels dueling
overhead showering twigs and fur.

I pirouette the blow downs and an adder forsakes his
shadow weaving toward me eager to sting. Gladly I
dance with him among the sterling sycamores, then,
knotting him around my throat in a broken necked
Windsor, trample star faces in the stream while a
trout savages my ankle.

Grouse, dreaming of eagles, stoop at wildcats and a
retired Morgan lounging in a hill pasture spies my
scent, races his terror among the broken apple trees
until the farmers below loose their dogs.
The hounds rush open-mouthed into my embrace.

Thanksgiving, 1970

In Bangkok you look for something beyond what you
came for and think you've found it for a while
because you need that something more. In the end
it's the same as New York, Seattle or Hono. Just
close your eyes and pump.

Untitled

I cannot bear the long pain farther, my skin jumping over the bloodless veins, blinking crusted eyes since the shuddered waking.

The moon is dulled, the wind speaks to others I hear flaming children, see black hair fanning a shattered skull.

Feet edge toward the soundless and eye-gouged dream. Among them once again.

American Son

I asked mama once. She said he was a GI.

The Tyranny of the Dead.

Standing lonely above them, their staring eyes shaming you, so recklessly erect.

You dare exhale, arrogant blood rushing, fleeing the malignant heart. Awkwardly alive, so temporary, fragile, the brain-bearing crown wrapped in steel despite futility. You feel the folly of persistence, a traitor to your calling, belted and strapped into the tools of trade, seeking bubbling lips, signals of failure you must pop once again, finish the trial.

Sloe-eyed dogs tentatively nose those waiting wrapping, dismayed by their own hunger, joining you in the guilt of the cognizant.

Zippo Inspection

I'd never heard that sound coming from a person or
anything before. Not of man or animal, but mythic,
the shrieking oarlocks of a black river crossing. A
comet fleeing God's humor I trapped and lashed to
kill the flames, or the sound.

The next day the parched, peeling skin of my fingers
felt newly born, unadjusted, horrified at the touch of
life.

The Farm

It wasn't much, just eighteen acres with the house in
front and two ponds and the woods in back; in
between half-a-dozen cows who had never thought of
stampeding.

The garage with woodshed tacked on back was to one
side of the house, then the fence and past it the green
tar-papered chicken house and the little white shack
where my great grandmother maintained her
independence.

On both sides of the chicken house it was wild and
tangled with blackberry briars where the banties
played that they were undomesticated.

The other lot was tamed; open and manicured except
for a bit of surliness along the fence line.

Jessa

She dances, the child and stamps in new shoes her joy, grinning out at life.

I hover near her, hope it's catching.

Erotica

The hand that halts my hand on her thigh is the same hand that keeps me from the medicine cabinet razor and its touch is as exciting as the place my hand wants to go.

Hong Kong Chinese Lady

I
At seventeen a shop worn barmaid with old mother and young brother to support. Though never a professional she apologized for having gone, as she put it, butterfly.

II
Lying together like friendly salmon at the bottom of a quick-stream she looked into my face wondering when I, like the rest, would leave.

III
She said I think I love you too much and she meant it but I left anyway.

Cat's Eyes

Sitting there across the table she looks at me with her walnut cat's eyes and I feel like a mouse bitten on the spine.

Oriental Hangup

Sitting in Chinatown
eating mushrooms and rice:
at last found a place in San Francisco
where I feel at home.
watching the young Chinese women pass,
wishing them into my life,
homesick for that part of the world
That has captured my soul
making me despair of hot dogs and round-eye women.

Guam, Christmas, 1972

Scrambling the rocks in salt streaked cutoffs he dances on coral and, booted against stonefish, crabwalks caressing with nervous fingers sprayholes and crevices springing at the small, chirping fish to feed his soul.

Choreographed with the surf he is recklessly careful stalking the reef-edge ghouled with sharks or perches, a grinning gargoyle on the lava boulder until the shadows sweep down the coast roaring, scattering fish and sunlight and he stands, heron-poised knee-deep in the tide pool below Tweed's Cave as they pass to sea bearing graves for school children and deacons.

Goose-skinned and timid he watches, oath-given to rescue on a weapons-issue planet clutching myriad-faced death between empty breasts giggling with the red-haired hungry.

Outhouse Thoughts

Out back, toward the hill,
among the cowpies and ash piles
is the outhouse.
An honest to Lil Abner, funky, Sears-Roebuck
one-holer outhouse.
I remember them from my extreme youth
before creeping middle class
saddled us with pipes and faucets
and flush handles.
And I discover during my first ritual labor
within those knot-holed, pine plank walls
that, after twenty years,
I'm still afraid of spiders in the hole.

No Dogs Or Indians Allowed

A goddamned bartender's sense of humor and too many beers to let it slide and I'm on my face in the slush in front of some back-ass Wyoming cowboy bar with knots on my skull because of a damned sign and a dog standing over me looking self-righteous.

Oakland Jacket

I got my leather coat at the Oakland Goodwill Store. It's a big, bulky, fleece-lined jacket that comes to the middle of my thigh like the ones bomber crews used to wear and was in good shape except for bullet holes in the left side of the chest which is probably why it was lying dead in a corner of a goodwill store. Haunted coats don't bother me so I bought it with my last five bucks and wore it next door to the Goodwill Kitchen for a bowl of free soup.

Bad Day

Some days just aren't worth a shit. They come in like sewage on the tide and you've got to wade through them like a city worker in hip boots.

Disaster

It's the sudden screaming silence that catches you, holds you bug on pin, that one that follows the smash-clash of Detroit steel; or certain screams or gunshots. Or when that child you've told 'be quiet' ten thousand times finally is. That shrilling shocked quiet as the whole listening world catches its breath. Then every dog in town starts barking and you run toward it yelling, 'What happened? What happened?'

Narcissism

Pacing the gray city
under a sky stricken with sparrows
I know that the only world is the one seen by my eye
and when that eye fails the world is lost.
There are no ideas but the buzzing
of my mind, no knowledge except that I carry.
What I've forgotten no longer exists, what I
remember is eternal.
Scribbling my way through this fool's errand,
scrawling on mangled bark chaptered nonsense with

footnotes and cites, I understand that the only real truth is that glimpsed in dreams and this must be forgotten. Remembering would throw God out of heaven.

New Hope Church, Bethesda, Arkansas

That church, hot and airless in August,
was heavy on condemnation and Hell,
sparse with forgiveness, redemption,
grace.
My first reason
for leaving the church was simple despair.
No one could be that good.

Religion 2

1
The only thing more difficult than believing in God is not believing in God.
2
Wrist or palm? Theologians fuss over this like old women nattering over fudge recipes. Through the palm or the wrist, as if it mattered a damn. If man does pass from the earth, it will come from nit-picking.
3
You can argue that the wandering preacher named Jesus only became Christ as the nails passed through his flesh and bit into the wood. That the hanging, beaten man with the lance in his side, who was still capable of love, was the Messiah. That the Christian church began when he cried for forgiveness rather than bloody vengeance

4

This brings me to a line of inquiry alarming, but evident. If Christ was born in the Crucifixion, was the Holocaust necessary to found Israel? Did it take a My Lai to finally drive the generals out of Vietnam? Must Jerusalem be slaughtered to enable the enlightenment? Does evil fuel good? Are good works a reaction to despair?

5

Must we squat in the fire before we can think to fetch water?

6

If there is a God, is it manifested in the forgiveness of survivors? I think of a woman who lived through My Lai describing horrors in an interview and saying she didn't hate Americans, but only wondered, why? Perhaps she, transcending hate, is why.

7

Grace comes through loving endurance.

Confession of a Race Traitor

Bio I

It was toward the end of the sixties, a bit after nineteen seventy – the sixties overlapped. Anyway, it was about the time we got tired of breaking things in Asia and came home. I was wearing a sailor suit and sitting in a hotel room just on the edge of Chinatown waiting out my second hitch, drinking beer and looking out at the street.

I was over four, had been places and seen things and was wondering if I would ever sleep well again. Without drinking that is. Enough beer and I slept like a baby.

I was still quite young, then. I'd been underage when I first enlisted, but didn't act young anymore. When I was nineteen a bar girl in Bangkok told me I acted like an old man.

Bio II

The boy I was died during the Vietnam War.
Everyone dies in a war, whether you walk away from
it or not. The child that enlists dies and what returns
is something else again.

I do miss him sometimes. He was a sweet child,
much nicer than I am, but he was silly and a fool. He
believed too easily, was naively jingoistic. He
swallowed it whole, a true believer. It's just as well
that he's gone.

Bio III

Years after the bankruptcy, somewhat after the
divorce, the writer was standing in the express lane of
a supermarket when a lady he knew only slightly
said, I hear you're writing a novel.

At the time he was writing, not sure if was a novel or
not, but in any case not talking about it. He used to
talk about writing a lot, but never got any done. Now
writing again, he never mentioned it and had no idea
how this lady knew, but was living in a small town
where people of vague acquaintance would speak of
secrets they shouldn't know.

He was holding, as he stood in the express lane, a
baby whose first name was the same as his and who
was no relation to him at all: the writer's mother's
step-grandson from a step-daughter who'd been
adopted in the first place. The baby's mother
wouldn't take care of him, the writer's mother
couldn't, so he ended up holding this baby in the

supermarket express lane while the son of his blood, object of his adoration lived thousands of miles away with a woman who periodically sent the writer long letters detailing exactly how much she hated him.

This is how life served him and is it any wonder that he's often confused and squints a lot?

Bio IV

I never mastered the tying of ties, either overhand or Windsor. During an enlistment in the United States Coast Guard I never learned to tie the neckerchief either and finally bought a cheater, a pre-tied knot through which the bitter ends are pulled. I can't find a cheater for civilian ties and have them tied by an understanding friend. They hang in my closet ready to slip over my head and be cinched tight like a collection of hangman's loops.

Memory

How do memories die anyway?

I used to have a memory, just one, of my father before the polio when he could walk. I started to write about it and in the writing realized it was gone.

I've a memory of a memory. I can recall the content and the emotions involved, but can no longer bring it to mind and see it again.

Do they just flicker out or grow nova-like expanding with dying energy to implode into nothing? One too many beers or an oxygen shortage caused by chain-smoking killed that one I guess; its loss spurred me to inventory what remains.

I can't remember my first wife's left breast. I do have a general idea of the kind of breast it was within a certain class of breasts; not too large, but quite nice really. She was a dancer with a wide-shouldered, athletic build, made her breasts seem smaller than they actually were.

She was a virgin when we married and I can't remember the look on her face when I first bulled past her vulva, nor can I remember exactly why I married her.

I can't remember my son's first step, but I still carry my great grand-father with me though he died when I was small, not long after my father's career as a biped ended. He still comes to mind sitting in his chair smoking a pipe and chewing tobacco simultaneously, a spit can at his feet, my great grandmother hovering like some benevolent harpy brushing errant coals off of his shirt.

Bio V

It can be instructive to witness what a man has not done.

The two best paying jobs I applied for and was offered were both jobs I finally could not accept.

One was with a city animal shelter where I would have divided my time between fetching and incinerating road kills and being the gas man. The other was with the CIA.

I did work in an emergency room, not in any healing way, but as a clerk interviewing patients. I clearly remember insisting that a woman who was carefully holding her eyeball in place give me her insurance information and being irritated by her distraction.

We all need grace.

Smile

Cheshire Cat faded away until only his grin remained. I'm still here and fleshier with age, but my grin has gone.

Looking at pictures the other day, some new ones of The Baby – you know the kind: here he is holding The Baby and there she is holding The Baby and here I am holding The Baby, but what caught me, in a moment of total self consciousness, was my own reflection on the film trying to smile for the camera.

I can't smile anymore. When I try, I grimace. I look like I have gas bad.

There's a couple of other shots, shots when I'm paying attention to The Baby and not the camera, not trying to smile and I look OK, not bad. Much better than those painfully pinched lips attempting to signal good cheer.

I looked back into some old photos, snapshots from long ago when I was a baby and a kid and in those days I mugged for the camera, grinning and acting out. In the photos of my father and I together Dad, more often than not, is frowning at me, disturbed by my monkeyshines.

The smile shrinks with time, you can see it. By the time I'm back from the 'service' (as my mother called it) it's a formal little thing as perfunctory and neatly groomed as my military mustache.

I can't find that point where I lost it completely. As you age you take fewer pictures of yourself. But it's gone now, that thing, gone for good and what it left behind is ugly, troubling and my latest resolution is, when the photographer says, 'smile,' to quietly leave the room.

Time Traveler

Some years ago I developed an aversion to the wearing of wristwatches and acquired one that rides in the pocket instead. An inexpensive yet durable Montgomery Ward special that survived, among other things, one trip through a washing machine and repeated thumpings when forgotten in the pocket of jeans thrown down at the end of day. After the washing machine incident its hunter's case lid closed crookedly, but close it did and the watch was honest about the time.

Awhile back for no apparent reason it gave up the ghost and laid in gold-plated death unable to wind, tick, or wave its hands. For over a year I have traveled without carrying time with me and discover that I still manage to make it to where I want to go.

Recently, traveling to a funeral, I crossed a time warp and regained an hour of my past making a day that, for me, was twenty-five hours long. Days later, returning along the same path, I lost an hour and so came out more or less even. After the trip I ran into another time-shift, this one legislated, and got my extra hour back, but in the spring it will be rescinded.

In 1973 I returned to North America from South Asia. I left Guam International Airport at 7:30 on a Friday and arrived in San Francisco at 7 p.m. the same day. While flying for fifteen hours with a customs stop in Honolulu, I traveled a half hour into the future.

Somewhere I have an ornate certificate attesting that I crossed the international dateline at sea. On this occasion the ship on which I was a crewman sailed into tomorrow, squatted there awhile for ceremonial purposes, then came back into today.

When I was a maritime radioman the exact time was a treasure. We would twice daily tune a special receiver to a laboratory in Colorado where scientists and wise men measured the earth's movements and tracked the stars and deduced from their calculations the exact time. They broadcast this to the faithful and we listened, standing at opened clocks, keys in hand, ready to capture and lock down the precise second.

Divorce

….?" You ask, before you remember that she's no longer there. As bad as it was the loss is still great scarring over, but tender yet, and as heavy upon you as original sin. An amputation of sorts; it takes a while to really understand that the member is gone.

The relief is wonderful, when the struggle is over, especially if you persevered, refused to relent, kept trying to knot the bitter ends after the line's rotted.
Like the man standing ready at the pumps when there's green water out the porthole, you are elated to finally get the hell out.

But the vessel's lost and you can't help, sitting in your room picking an album with no one's opinion to consider but your own, catching a chill.

Environmental Impact Statement

There were three cats waiting for me that morning: all marled gray and of a size, obvious litter mates.

The first one showed up a couple of days ago and I fed him. He came back, I fed him again and now I think he's taken up living in one of the sheds out back. That morning he brought his siblings and I fed them too.

Then I hanged the bird feeder, that skirmish line where the starlings chase the sparrows and the squirrels chase the starlings, a bit higher if only to feel better and I already have a tin guard on the birdhouse post.

As everywhere, life isn't a sure thing in my backyard. One does what they can, but cannot provide guarantees.

This whole business of birds, cats and squirrels upsets my Airedale; he trembles with restraint. He knows better than to do anything in his own backyard, but he is a terrier and his idea of proper treatment for small animals is to shake them until they die.

Insomnia

One of those nights. Sleep is so far away that, like sex, you can't really remember what it was like.

You lay in bed listening to the thud of blood in your mind, counting the pulse beats mildly wondering what you would do if it stopped and you were still conscious and laying there in the silence until your brain died.

It's chastening to be so totally dependent on a simple muscle. You remember all the abuse you've handed it with strong drink, tobacco, fried eggs; you're not so young anymore. You remember how grandpa dropped dead and think it could seize up any moment and all the thoughts and dreams, goods and evils, hopes and fears; all the bewildering complexities dangling by that pulsating bit of flesh would be gone. If it falters a world is lost.

I'm an uneasy sleeper. I feel entirely vulnerable and it makes me nervous. I was a poor child growing up in elderly and ill-used houses that, when the lights were out and all abed, creaked and complained through the night. The noises terrorized me. I didn't understand then and thought the madman was coming. All small children know that there is a madman with a long knife out to kill them and my thought at every groan of the plank floor was, "here he is."

Later I grew up and my fears were confirmed.

I'm older now and not frightened by every vagrant noise, but I also know damned good and well that the madman really is out there. He's not after me personally and the odds of his picking my window are slim, but he's real.

I sleep with a pistol and flashlight, my torch and sword against the darkness. It's not that I entertain fantasies of midnight duels: I don't want to shoot the madman. The gun is just company on a long night listening to my heartbeat and waiting for him to pass by.

Insomnia II

I have lost, somewhere in the years, the ability to easily fall asleep. I lay in bed weighted with my usual fatigue and can feel sleep coming, a thickening, my brain setting up like mortar, thought becoming heavy and slow when a slight noise from the street, a louder tick of the clock will crack my torpor into complete alertness and I must wait through the whole process again. Doesn't always need outside interference either. Often my brain will, at the last possible edge of consciousness, snap itself back to reality as if afraid of the dark. I use the word snap because it seems to me that I actually hear a snapping like the breakage of overstressed nylon line. And at this sudden awareness my numbed thoughts, which as they slowed seemed also to become less rigid and more inventive, caught halfway on their journey to becoming dreams, scramble maniacally under the blasting light like roaches in a midnight kitchen, making designs I'd never suspected.

A great big girl tightly wrapped in screaming red and orange stretch fabric, a K-Mart special blouse and shorts set that cut so deeply into the loose, doughy flesh it was painful to see.

I was down at the playground watching my daughter manipulate the intricate caste system there when this girl arrived, walking past me with her mouth agape and revealing teeth with little experience of dentistry and none of orthodontry.

She was pale, pale with zinc white legs coming out of her flaming shorts, a thin thatch of blonde-brown hair crowning her hair and her pimpled, flat face, heavily plastered over with flesh toned Clearisil, was the most color she had, barring the clothes.

She was so desperately unattractive she made me think again that homeliness, in this land where white teeth, regular features and a flat belly are so much more important than scholarship or character, should be considered a disability. Her great, unattractive first impression must be a handicap of some kind. I admit, with great guilt, that, being unattractive myself in a short, slight Mr. Peepers way, that she was the kind of person I could look at and feel better about myself. She might have the soul of an angel and a mythic hero's courage, but would anyone ever in her life take the trouble to venture past the façade and find this out?

She pushed a stroller with one hand and carried a baby carrier in the other and this heartened me: at least she had known love, if only the physical and been able to bear fruit. She had her babies and I didn't look for a wedding ring; that was none of my business.

At the swing set she set the carrier down and began getting her babies out and I saw they were dolls; big, pink plastic baby dolls with mouths in a permanent pout and painted blonde hair, blue eyes. Identical dollies naked but for diapers and the big girl placed them, back to back in a baby swing, four rubber legs poking through the holes, blank eyes looking out.

She swung them then, pushing them gently. She didn't coo to the dolls or say anything, but silently stood pushing at the swing like it was one more chore to be done. If she was having fun, she hid it well and I sat watching this thinking this is where we should be looking for treasures, mysteries to solve. To hell with space and unexplored lands and the ocean's bottom; this huge girl's life, this business with the dolls is all the mystery I need. Solve her story and the meaning of life will be easy meat.

Libido Lament

Every time I think I've finally gotten past it, have found peace at last, poor peter resurrects himself, wakes me in the night to bully me some more.

Asian women always do it. No matter how quiet he's been I can't walk through Little Saigon without my blood pounding and scalding my skin, poor peter spreading his hood.

I've tried not to reproduce, however; took steps to avoid that. Why should I father children to play parts in the sad charade? Chances are someone will arrange for my sons to have a war in which they must shoot or get shot.

There is tragedy at both ends of the gun.

Or a daughter to stand and watch as the troops come to town, her only defense to smear herself with ashes and shit, to be interrogated with a wire from her vulva to a jeep's battery while an aroused and acned boy pumps the accelerator?

Disability

My war wound is the roaring in my ears. Irreparable nerve damage caused by inescapable noise: blasts and shots and explosions and screams. I passed through the firestorm untouched, but cannot stop listening to it.

It's worse sometimes than others depending on mood, background noise, alcohol abuse. Some days my hearing is nearly normal and on others I can hear nothing outside my head.

There are frequencies, those in the higher scale that I never hear: certain telephones, truck's backing and my son's chirping words when he first learned to speak.

"What?" I said over and over to the little boy dancing with rage.

Confession Of A Race Traitor

I've got a good Anglo-Saxon name except that it's not mine.

It's the name of my great grandmother's second husband who adopted my grandfather and gave it to us all. My real name has gotten misplaced over the years. No one mentioned it and then they were all dead. Rumor has it was German-Jew.

An ethnic cocktail anyway. Raised as a white man in a time (pre-civil rights) and a place (the American south) that it mattered a great deal, I'm a goodly part non-white (native American) and part somewhere in between (Jewish).

There have been numerous times when I've witnessed the work of white men and clung tightly to my non-white parts saying, "I'm not one of them."

I formally gave up being a white man in 1973 on moral grounds; quit being an American and a Christian too, for the same reasons. Went ethnic and cosmic for a time calling myself a Hebrew/Indian resident of the planet Earth, but don't worry about such things too much anymore; pass time without religion or politics.

I still think nationalism is a mistake, but travel on an American passport without qualm. It's necessary and it's the one I was issued. I just don't think it should give me a break on the ticket.

Nowadays when it comes up I term myself just one more Homo sapiens sapiens variegated.

A hooker I knew in Bangkok took me to visit her son, showing me a snap of the father, some Chicano GI. She compared her black hair to his, their similar olive skins and said, "Mexican same same Thai."

I agreed not to be polite, but from a simple and profound belief that we are all same same Thai.

Reality

I once believed in things, the usual, but received a crash course in reality in Cochin China. Of course the reality there was something else and here one must be subtler or altogether more brutal.

A new reality.

They used to talk, times gone by, about altering reality. About using acid and dope to make life more reasonable, but it seems to me that more often reality is a shape-shifter, changing itself, and we must scramble to fit it.

Reality is a dream. Each man divines his own, then warps the situation to fit it.

Two statements at odds, yet each absolutely true. Here's where simple minds come to grief, the inability to understand that things can be true while giving the lie to each other.

Fuck reality. I've given it up.

At a time when reality was machine gun fire directed at brown-eyed agrarian people by blue-eyed merchants I decided to leave that and all subsequent realities and turn instead to strong beer and the dreams it inspires.

For a while I let myself be influenced by others' expectations, but finally returned to the truth, as I know it. I've never regretted that choice.

Perchance To Dream

Every once in a while I just have to drink beer. I don't mean have a beer or two watching TV or listening to music. I mean sitting down with a case in the refrigerator with drinking as the focus of the evening. Using beer as a means to getting to the point where I can giggle and beyond to a little temporary oblivion. It is beer drinking as a faith whose prime tenant is that all human endeavor is a crock and you might as well have some beers and a laugh.

I guess it's a sixties sort of thing I've pulled down through all the years.

One of my big problems in life is that I believe this. It's really the way I feel. I've experienced business and academics and worked in hospitals and in the military. I've been a sailor and a soldier and a clerk and a scholar and it's all a crock. I must, to fulfill my obligations in life, pretend an interest. It's like when your son comes up with a picture he's drawn full of blood and death and wants to tell you who's the good guy and who's bad and why they are doing this to each other and you must pretend to take it seriously or hurt his feelings. So I, to avoid hurting the feelings of those people who care about me, pretend to take it seriously.

But it wears me out and sometimes I just have to drink beer. I don't drink much anymore; I once drank heavily every day, but now I hardly touch booze. It's been over a year since I've had a drink of anything, but I know my endurance will flag and I'll have to drink beer and giggle and sleep. And awaken the next morning sick and looking into the face of the years ahead of me wishing that it mattered.

A Mortal Replies

"I drink not to mock God, or for the love of wine,
but only to forget myself for awhile."
                                    Omar Khayyam

Why do you drink? Why should I not? I drink so that I can smile for a change; forget, sleep, all of this in a lovely stupidity that newspapers and anchormen can't touch.

I love cigarettes too; short, non-filtered Lucky Strikes that seem to appear lit and half-smoked in my fingers. And fresh side pork and over easy eggs and white bread fried in grease.

One must die after all. No matter how many miles one runs or how much grain one eats or how much joy one surrenders, death will come.

It makes me weary, all this attention to the body. It is in this that the brain atrophies. I weaken. I cannot run a mile, but where is there to run? By death we are snared; further flight is futile. We bide our time, try to smile.

Manifest Destiny

I

Christians

1

I take pen in hand this year of their Lord nineteen
hundred and ten to relate the fearful and grievous tale
of the renegade savage who spread terror and blood
across the high desert of Oregon state.

Being said savage:

My name
            Not my name really but the white
            name I was issued at the Hendricks
            Academy along with a hair cut and
            long pants
is Lionel Christian.

            Yes, I do appreciate the irony of
            this name though I'm certain the
            flour-faced fools who gave it did
            not.

I do not know my father or mother, or the people I
came from:

They are all dead.

I do not know my home or,
> as the CHRISTIANS would put it
> having drawn lines on paper and
> split the world into packets,
the state of my birth,

The masters of the academy would not tell me anything. My memories would not serve them. I came too young to carry my own and what they could have given me, they denied. They did not want me to have a past that might impede my development as an educated, CHRISTIAN gentleman.

> And, of course, they might not have
> known. The history of a savage is
> irrelevant.

I know not my people's name or their tongue, but I heard rumors, stories that I was of the Diggers, the basin Indians who ate insects and worms. That my people had eaten a CHRISTIAN's cow and had been killed for this crime.

Sometimes the story was that I, a babe at the time, was the only one allowed to live. Others said that more children had been spared, perhaps brothers and sisters.

At the academy we were Indians and our job was to become not Indians. We were to become CHRISTIANs except we could never be real CHRISTIANs because we were Indians. It is, I believe, somewhat akin to original sin.

We were expected to spend our lives attempting the salvation of civilization while living with and constantly reminded of the fact that we were condemned to barbarity.

Our masters at the academy knew that their task was impossible, but it was their service to their god to struggle in vain. Each day they strove to make us in their image and waited for us to fail.

2

Miss Holzberg, my employer: five feet tall and skinny, wizened to the bone. About forty I guess and pale. She stayed indoors for fear of the sun. She covered herself everyday in earth-toned clothes from chin to toes, layers of wool and cotton and never bathed or washed her teeth. She considered the one practice immodest and the other a fad. She chewed cloves both to temper her breath and against the pain of her rotten teeth. And she laved herself in perfume so that years before her death she smelled of sweet decay.

I was her clerk. I sold from behind the counter and handled anything that needed writing or calculations as Little Fisher, the other employee, and Holzberg herself were illiterate. Little Fisher, who wouldn't or couldn't speak and was simple, did the fetching and stocking wares on the shelves and the loading or unloading of wagons. When I needed something from the stockroom and was too busy to get it myself, I had to have Miss Holzberg tell Little Fisher to go as even a dumb moron would bridle at being ordered about by an Indian. I was given a bunk in a little storage room off of the kitchen and next to the outhouse. I often wondered about the proximity of the well to the dung pit, tried not to think about it when I drank my morning coffee. On hot nights sleep was impossible in the stench and I would go sleep in the stable. Curious how the smell of horse shit is rich and of the earth while man's is simply foul.

Hiring me, having an Indian about, was Holzberg's penance, her substitution for beating her back with chains and she also profited from it, at least for the first few months I was there. Her customers, the simpletons who worked the surrounding ranches, men too dull for any work but the care of dumb animals, would ride long miles to buy a plug of tobacco and see the tame Indian. And drink whiskey, which I sold them though it was against the law for me to take a drink myself.

The population of Spencer would swell then from its normal total of three. These cowboys, stupid as the animals they lived with and often, truth be told, coupled with, would drain one bottle and then another until they collapsed. Miss Holzberg had built a livery and dormitory with wooden shelves for bunks. She would have Little Fisher put the drunkards in one, their mounts in another, and charged for both.

3

The other day I took a ride along the river
         at least it's a river when it rains
to let the wind blow away the dreams of murder in my brain and some miles east of town came upon death.

Nothing unusual around here,
> something is always rotting in the grass

but this was remarkable in its number. There must
have been thirty or so assorted animals:
> buzzards and juncos and crows,
> black-faced weasels and coyotes and big-

eared foxes, all in a circle radiating from the bloated
carcass of a steer. The steer, sick from this or that,
must have come this way to die by the water and then
someone stuck poison in him. Long standard practice
to kill wolves, but whoever baited this beef was
dreaming.
> If there are any wolves
> left in the world they surely aren't
> around here. The last wolf was
> trapped or shot or blasted out of this
> state a decade past.

I spend much time along the riverbank trying to learn
the language of the planet.

The tales are written by beasts: their tracks and piss
stains and turds are the headlines, the agony columns,
the scriptures of the earth.

> For me it might as well be Sanskrit.

I can read Latin and Greek. I'm familiar with the
bloated self-importance of those old pirates, their
shoulders perched with gods instead of parrots. I
know the names of dead kings and moldering popes.

I know how Cromwell died and what Cotton Mather
thought. I'm as stuffed with CHRISTIAN history as
a Christmas goose with chestnuts, but I cannot read

the signs beneath my nose, have no idea of what passed here.

I do not know my father's name or the song my mother sang me and if I want to curse my enemies without using their hateful tongue I can find no words but only howl.

I have read that in the far north and to the south in Amazonas there are Indians still beyond the reach of drummers and priests: Indians living in the old way, who still hunt and tend their fires and know their fathers, who have escaped the slavery of the children of that sad-eyed Jew, but if I have read of them, then they are known and their destruction is assured.

4

         Indians, Hindus, Chinamen,
they pin their god to us with bayonets. Those not shot or hanged or burned on their priested pyres they chain with whiskey-tobacco-sugar and the madness of gold.

To live we must ape their lunacy, mouth their words, strive in their image.

         Indians, Hindus, Chinamen.
         They make niggers of us all.

There was a Chinaman in Rosemon, who, one day, perhaps thinking about never having a woman, began cutting off his fingers. He removed all those on the left hand and realized he could not now cut off the fingers of his right, so he thrust that hand into the stove and burned it off at the wrist. He then decided to kill himself, but couldn't manage it without hands. He asked his friend, another Chinaman with whom he operated a laundry, for help and his friend strangled him.

When it was discovered the CHRISTIANS grabbed their ropes and came for the surviving Chinaman.

Killing a Chinese was
no great crime
for a CHRISTIAN, but you couldn't
let a celestial son get away with it.

They had the fellow strung up and kicking when someone mentioned that there would be no one left to do the laundry now. The champions of justice amended their sentence and lowered the Chinaman to cough his way back to life and bury his friend.

It's said that he is still there, doing the wash for the men who hanged him, little damaged except that the rope crooked his neck and it stiffened that way so that his head sits horizontally on his shoulders.

5

It was not my degrading slavery to Miss Holzberg that caused me to kill her. I do not want to be misunderstood, though sharing her bed would certainly drive most men to murder. She died because she was there at the beginning of my war and was of the enemy.

Nothing personal.

It was her forced embrace that convinced me that the war was to be waged; that illustrated my doom and crushed my nose into it like a spaniel's into a soiled carpet.

I refused her at first spinning a tale of religious commitment and celibacy to spare her feelings on that close day in the airless store, its windows nailed shut against dust and night vapors. And she brought her face with it's shark's fin nose up to mine and spat out the words with her spiced and fetid breath.

> "If you don't do what I want you to do I
> will tell them that you did do it and they
> will hang you from the windmill."

I did what she wanted amazed as I did so that I was able. She was bony and hairy and smelled of the outhouse, but the will to live is strong in the young and my manhood would summon itself to appease her sour aperture.

After that the mechanical moaning of the windmill, once only an irritation on the periphery of the ear, became the knelling of my death bell.

                    The wild Indians were gone
and the wolves
                    were dead and one close day
deviled by their
                    complaining   wives   and
quarrelsome children
                    and all the days of labor left
before them

beating a horse would not be
enough. A
plague would decimate their
flocks or a
well go dry and they would
remember there
was one Indian left. I knew
that I would
one day end up dangling from
their tower
as nothing more than a
midsummer diversion.

6

CHRISTIANS are always surprising. I had expected Miss Holzberg to die spitting, but with the entry of the knife she fell straight down dead, almost gently, her only protest the grimace on her face.

Little Fisher found his tongue with my ax in his skull. Cursing and yelling he reached for me, his spirit finally rising as I split his brainpan and the sun shone in on his thoughts. I had to open his head and beat his spirit to death while he snatched at my ankles and tried to bite me. When it was finished the top of his head was destroyed, his face swollen, congested, sunburn red as if scorched by his passion of strength.

The cowboy, a passerby, used to bunking in rough housing with drunks and idiots, had slept through Fisher's screams. I merely poked my rifle through the window and shot and shot him in his bed. He settled lower among his sougans and that was that.

This was the massacre at Spencer and when it was over I replaced the bullet fired into the cowboy, wiped Fisher off of my ax and cleaned my knife. Then I sat on the steps outside Holzberg's and smoked my pipe. It was a hot, summer day stilled by the sun, even the dust too worn out to stir and there was a peace to the place with only Little Fisher's body outside the stable to show that murder had been done.

> I had often wondered what was in a
> CHRISTIAN's head, what compulsion to
> Shackle themselves to their little
>   Squares of dirt, to worship their
>   Condemning god, to wall themselves
>   In their breathless houses with the
>   Knowledge of Hell and think themselves
>   king. I walked over to Little Fisher
>   and took a long look into his, but found
>   no secrets there. His brain looked no
>   different than a pig's.

7

The state militia came, a patrol of
heroes in the brand-new, stiff khakis
with old, long-tom Springfield rifles
that, slung in short boots from their
cantles, dragged their muzzles along
the ground.

But only half a dozen. The rest must
still be milking or egg hunting or lying
abed pizzle in hand wondering if they'll
ever find out what lies up a woman's

dress snce the few white women won't
and there aren't any Indian women left
to rope and we lie too far north for
senoritas.

I tied my horse in the open knowing that,
when sighted, the fools would ride directly
to it, and crouched nearby behind a rock.

I'm certain the the CHRISTIAN newspapers
have called this a battle and so I will describe
this savage duel between the militia and the
crazed aborigine.

At about twenty-five yards, as they neared as
if on parade, I opened fire. Four of them stopped
their animals and attempted to pull their
buffalo rifles and I shot them dead more
quickly than I can write it down.

I'm not bragging about my shooting. At
that distance with a modern rifle it's no
great feat to put a shot in the center of a
man's chest and with my little .303 Savage
and soft-pointed bullets, a strike in the
chest is death. Sitting there, trying to
pull their bean-pole rifles free, they gave
me all the time in the world.

At rifle crack two of the brigade remembered
their obligations and spurred their horses for
home. I ignored one, someone must spread
the news, but I mounted and pursued the
other.

His rifle rattled and dug into the ground. He Lashed to both sides with a quirt, sometimes whipping the horse, sometimes himself, and kicked his feet so high in spurring that he looked like an acrobat. As I drew nigh he looked back and I could see his lips moving.

I could smell him (sweat and odure) and I could smell his horse (just sweat) and all the equipment hung from the harnessing clattered and groaned like a graveyard of ghouls.

I struck him from the saddle with my ax.

"John, oh John," he said to me.

He didn't try to rise or run or fight. He lay, his back bleeding from my blow, and said, "John, oh John."

I fed him my ax.

I disjointed him not from malice, but to make it simpler for the coyotes to fetch away a meal. I was about to remove his head when whimsy caught me and instead I looped my lariet around his neck and set out trailing the trooper, less his limbs, along behind.

That evening, about an hour before the local was due, I set him up between the rails of the trunk line between Burton and Cassell facing in the direction from which the train would come and left him to plead with the steam engine.

8

I am befuddled.

So many years I lived swollen with the desire, the need to kill CHRISTIANS only to find my own deeds sicken me. There is no joy.

These great murderers must only, I thought, understand protests written in blood, but I underestimated their stupendous madness. It's the most amazing thing about them, makes them blind and deaf to the world, overwhelms all understanding. Even I, their lunacy's child, cannot fully comprehend it.

The world will die of it.

> At the Stoller ranch I tried to drink blood caught in   bucket when I cut the fat girl's throat, but it outraged my stomach.
> I had my little joke of building a fire and Leaving a partially cooked arm on the spit so that the CHRISTIANS could have their nightmare, but what the godless cannibal ate was in truth thrown to the coyotes and I didn't laugh.

The beast of the high desert relents, oh my. Closer indeed to the beasts than the CHRISTIANS I find myself as a beast soon has his belly full and goes away. The CHRISTIANS never say enough.

There is some pleasure in this discovery.

The question is what next? I'm not a very good Indian. I can't hunt for beans. Without the CHRISTIANS to kill and stead from, I'll starve. Though I hate them, they must feed me so am I not, even with their blood between my teeth, just another of their niggers?

I can't live in the way of my fathers (Who were they? What was their names?) and I can't be a CHRISTIAN so I find myself in the world with no ledge on which I can perch.

> They have taken what we were and won't let us be what they are, so we are without and no one knows what to do.

> Who wants to be a CHRISTIAN? To climb aboard that wild horse and ride it to the end of time? Not I nor anyone with sense, so the problem is to think of something else to do.

I had thought, one time, to catch myself a tame Indian woman and breed her, fire my rage into her womb and bring forth another CHRISTIAN killer, but gave that up for the foolishness it was. Such a child would probably grow up normal, which is to say he would spend his days slaving for the CHRISTIANS hoping to make enough money to dress and live like the CHRISTIANS do.

One more nigger.

> Instead I'm going to take my poke of rations from the Stoller ranch (bacon, flour, a can of tomatoes) and walk into the desert to wait for

visions and look for God's face. I want a word with him. I'll take with me the pleasure of knowing that for months to come random night noises will squeeze the CHRISTIANS' innards with fear and they'll think of me.

Perhaps that's all I can hope for.

II

The Black Meo

I

I went hunting with Shoob, a man in his thirties who I much admired. He had two wives and five children and the ability to love them all.

He was also a fine hunter with the grace to let me stumble along, queering his stalks and alarming the jungle with my pungent farang smell.

At the end of eighteen months when I packed my notes to leave he said to me in Thai, "Now you know all my secrets."

In my western arrogance I believed him.

II

Consider this a confession.

I am a man responsible for the death of a people, the destruction of a culture.

This is frequently done by missionaries and still is (God's work), but I was an anthropologist, a student of culture and you would think I would have known better.

Not that I meant to cause the diaspora of the Black Meo. In the words of fools everywhere, it was an accident.

III

You must undestand what a treasure the Black Meo were to me. A new people. To do the first major investigation of an ethnic group was to secure your career, make your fortune. And by the nineteen sixties it was impossible.

Everyone was found. Everyone had been examined. Looking for unknown people was as rewarding as searching Loch Ness.

I was working on the Kuomontang, the Chinese army units that retreated south into the hills of Burma, Laos and Thailand when the communists took over and found mention of the Black Meo. I looked further and found a reference there, a cite here, but no real work. The most information I could find in one place was a few sentences in a monograph published by the Burmese government on the involvement of ethnic groups in the opium trade.

It became apparent that there was no ethnic study of the Black Meo in the west. It was like wandering through a salvage yard and stumbling over the one true cross.

IV

I went to the anthropology department for help in finding funding and it was forthcoming: a generous grant awarded by the Western Institute of Eastern Studies, a group I understood was loosely under the aegis of the State Department. They wanted a monthly summary of my notes, alinguistic survey, complete ethnohistory and copies of all collected material.

V

The Black Meo were a hill tribe in that part of Asia now famous as the Golden Triangle. Like most hill tribes, they came from somewhere else and ended up where more numerous peoples had pushed them. A wasteland people in the rocky, jungled hills where rice wouldn't grow. They learned to grow yams for food and opium for profit and to love their mountains.

They grew tobacco and smoked hand-rolled cigarettes using leaves for paper. They wore blue cotton shirts with ties rather than buttons and carried bush knives in basketry sheaves at their backs.

They grew opium and those who smoked it did so in long pipes of beaten silver. These pipes, hung by brightly colored and tasseled cords from the left shoulder, were part of their formal dress whether they actually smoked opium or not. Formal dress was of heavy black cotton with ornate appliqués of red and yellow.

VI

Young men courting wore orchids and stuffed birds in their hair and played love songs on wooden flutes.

VII

Opium smoking was considered an activity for the elderly, generally men aged beyond work though some women took up the habit. Opium use by the young or family men was considered dissipation. For the most part opium was a male activity, betel nut being used by women. Both sexes were fond of beer.

VIII

The Black Meo had been hunters and were hunters still for food and additional income and Simply because they were hunters. They hunted small game with tangle nets, figure four deadfalls, blowpipes and crossbows. With muzzleloaders and the occasional breech-loading shotgun they hunted gaur and banteng. They also hunted barking, hog-nosed and sambar deer, mountain goats (tahr) and wild boar for food. They hunted tiger and leopard where these still occurred for their hides and the medicinal qualities given to parts of the cats' bodies. They hunted Asian black bear with spears for sport and as a test of courage. They considered the bear the most savage beast in their forest.

They didn't hunt the elephant or golden wildcat. Both were considered creatures of good fortune. The golden cat, fire tiger in their dialect, was often kept in captivity and its fur was a specific for burns.

The hamarydad or king cobra was captured alive and held to be slaughtered when needed for medicinal use. Their folk medicine attributed great healing power to the snakes' gall bladders.

There were shamans among the Black Meo and female shamans or witches. And seers and mediums. Ghosts were believed in and dealt with as part of daily life. The Black Meo believed that their dead remained close around them. They were animists, believers in nature spirits and though they personified some of these spirits, their animism was less a matter of worship than a simple respect for the essence of the mountains, trees, beasts and those people who had lived before them. Some adopted Buddhism, but only as an addition to their animism, not as a replacement.

IX

The last information I ever gathered on the Black Meo was a copy of a MACV report given me by a man I met in Lucy's Tiger Den in Bangkok.

It described the Black Meo as brave in battle, fierce as Gurkhas when the spirit was in them, but too whimsical and fey for good military discipline. They made reasonable guerilla fighters, were poor and willing to fight for pay. They were politically naïve.

Linguistically the Black Meo were connected to the Yurgiff and other Mongol-Siberian peoples. Physically they were a stout, round-headed, full-faced people reminiscent of northern Asian groups.

They loved the mountains and now they are gone.

X

I don't know if it was the CIA or the Army Intelligence Service or the Office of Navy Intelligence. Or SOG or CISO or MACV. Or the Australians wanting some influence in the area or the French wanting to get some back. Or any combination of these groups or any number of them working separately.

It doesn't matter from whence they came, the agents with bribes and propaganda and cajolery to involve the Black Meo in the anti-communist crusade. The intelligence they used was from me.

XI

It didn't take long; there weren't that many Black Meo to begin with. About the time it takes a man to finish a dissertation and defend it. To receive a master's and accept a position as a research associate. To rework the dissertation into a proper preliminary ethno history and have it published by a university press. To write a popular version and have that published as well. Abut the time it takes a bookish man with no outside interests to do these things along with a good start on a Phd, say three years, and the Black Meo no longer existed.

A few individuals still lived, but as a cultural unit, the Black Meo had been destroyed. Adult males of military age had been eliminated: there were none left unmaimed and alive. Within three years an uncrippled Black Meo male was either a grandfather or a child. Their land, the rocky uplands no one else in history had wanted suddenly became valuable. The communists wanted it and the anti-communists wanted it and the Black Meo fled under waves of bombers that did not consider indigenous populations. While the men died in the war their dependents languished in camps outside the capital and later across the river in Thailand.

By the time I returned to Asia, shortly after the United States decided it had no further business there, they were gone. The men were dead, the elderly dispersed among camps, the children adopted by barren Europeans and the young women servicing tourists in Bangkok.

XII

The dust is what I remember most.

I'd heard a rumor that some of the tribe's survivors, loose family groups, were scuttling between free fire zones, squatting in hidden nooks and reverting as best as they could to normal life until the war found them again. Some of these could be Black Meo.

Chasing another story, one of those half-answers you get there with a shrug and a smile, I had gotten into the highlands in a Japanese jeep with a Thai driver using a variety of university IDs and a couplemail order press cards to manipulate the various policemen and soldiers trying to turn me back.

A valley between jungled ridges. About a mile wide, the floor remarkably flat and unfeatured except for a stream down its center. Perhaps a canal. It seemed too direct and unbending to be natural. Dirt tracks paralleled the stream bed on either side. Across from me a shambled sheet-tin shed, perhaps an abandoned shop, and a woman walking in the dust, the only person in the valley besides us in the jeep.

I wanted to talk to her, to ask my incessant questions, and walked toward her. I had to cross the streambed and was down there when the first bombs hit.

XIII

I'd never been bombed before and don't know if this was typical or not. The sky was solid cloud cover from ridgetop to ridgetop. I saw no aircraft, heard no warning whistle. The plain around me just began erupting, the earth throbbing beneath my feet.

A shrill crack, a basso roar, a rush of heated air. Swellings of red dust and gray-black smoke with hearts of flame. And then, insistent through the roaring, loud in my ringing ears, I heard whistles and whispers and whinings. This was shrapnel, those little bits of metal exploding bombs whip out.

For a moment I was overshadowed, something passing overhead. At the time I had an impression of an aircraft or some great bird, but now I think it must have been some part of the abandoned shop.

I ran in the direction I was facing, away from the jeep, toward the shop. Not a thought in my head. No ideas of finding cover or hiding, just running.

The hole was there and I fell into it. Otherwise I would have kept running across the valley and either made it or not, but the hole was there and I fell into it and onto the woman.

XIV

The dust: at each detonation the earth spewed clotted clouds of red dust like arterial bleeding. In the hole I could barely see and only realized I was stop the woman when I inadvertently grasped her breast, felt the nipple against my fingers with the heart's flutter underneath. My nose was choked shut and I gasped open-mouthed, mud caking my tongue.

I pulled away from her as far as I could (even in a bombardment an Asian woman would be offended by over-familiarity) and saw a woman in either late youth or early middle age looking at me with that expression which says nothing, but is just there, and a hole in her face.

A small hole (half a dime) beside her nose. Little bleeding, nearly none and the hole was clean, by which I mean it was not ragged, but surgically neat. Not a round hole, but rather a rounded triangle.

I didn't know if I should try somehow to bandage the wound; she seemed to be breathing through it. Moist whistles.

And you never know about head wounds. A scalp wound, for example, always bleeds like hell and you must burrow down through the thick, black hair not knowing if you will find scratched skin or brain tissue.

XV

I wetted a handkerchief with spittle, the only moisture available besides sweat or urine, and dabbed at the dust around the wound, then used it to give her a mask against the dust, covering her face beneath the watching eyes.

The nearer explosions heaved the earth and tossed us like dice in a cup. My one firm notion of first aid is that the injured should be kept still and, disregarding convention, I embraced the woman, wrapped my arms and legs around her trying to give her my body as an anchor, but it was no good. The bombs were stronger than I and in a lover's clasp we flew in our hole.

Sense left me and, though I was conscious, I knew nothing. I don't remember when the bombing ended. I remember realizing that the woman seemed to have stopped blinking. It was over then, I don't know for how long. I pulled the mask away and looked for respiration, but the hole was silent. I tried to lick my fingertip, but could no longer produce saliva. I spat dust and finally found some moisture inside my lower lip. With my wetted fingertip I gently touched her fixed eye and knew I was alone.

XVI

I tried to close her eyes as I'd seen done in movies, but they wouldn't stay shut. In the end I laid the handkerchief over her face.

Out of the hole I started to walk away, then returned. I couldn't leave her lying in an open pit. It was the notion of flies finding her that bothered me. I have for some time had a horror of flies. I once watched a man smoking a cigarette while flies walked on his brain. So I kicked and pulled at the dry dirt and interred her.

Of the jeep I found one wheel with a piece of axle attached. Of the driver, absolutely nothing.

III

The Last Medicine Man

I

Down in the hollow the mountain feist is short-haired with half a tail.

He enjoys killing and spends much time chasing small animals, shaking their tiny, squeaking lives out of them, in the blackberry tangles along the old fence line. He comes in briar-torn happy, stained with blood both his own and his prey's.

We, the feist and I, live in an old 31 foot Airstream travel trailer. It was last the office of a used car lot and was bare except for a desk and a toilet. I had a shower put in and a kitchen sin, propane stove and a regular refrigerator (they've put in electric down here), had it moved down the hollow, put a foundation under it and knocked the wheels off intending to go no farther.

The hollow is about a quarter mile wide, flat-bottomed with wooded slopes rising sharply on both sides. Vision is limited here, the sky reduced to a ribbon. I'm hoping the hills will block distractions and night terrors as they do TV transmissions. I've spent too much time in dreams lately, came here to clear my mind.

My walls are lined with books. Some of them have accompanied me on my travels and some were my father's, but most are new, acquired as my queries led me in unexpected directions toward unknown destinations. I have traveled to university bookstores for them and sent through the mail. They fill my rough shelves and sit in stacks on the floor.

You start with a question and never know where you'll end up. This is my present and final journey.

II

In 1982, after my second hitch, after my second marriage I was working for a window installer out of Denver, Colorado. The company put windows into new buildings; hard work and often high up which scared me, but sometimes it's good to be scared and it paid well.

I spent my nights in a bar frequented by American Indians from a variety of tribes attracted to Denver as rural people are attracted to cities everywhere. One night a Southern Cheyenne I'd gotten to know began to tell me about a fellow he'd met when he lived in Minneapolis. The old man was the last pure blood survivor of a tribe related to the Paiutes, Great Basin Indians, and he was a shaman, a magician in the tradition of a tribe that no longer existed.

Word had gotten around that I was an anthropologist and these guys would have their stories for me, usually bogus, wild stuff just putting the white man on, but this Southern Cheyenne was too sad for games and he had the old man's address in Minnesota. I copied the address, but was only mildly interested. American Indians weren't my specialty and I wasn't a practicing anthropologist anymore. I'd given that up years ago. Then I got sick and was in the hospital for a while, took another job, got buried and came into money.

III

After one set of doctors told me it was all in my head, another set of doctors told me I wasn't crazy, just nervous, hyper sensitive. After they had rested me for a time I was released and went to work for a company that put in septic tanks. My job was to go down in the hole when the backhoe was done and shovel out the tailings and I was down in a hole doing this when the earth sighed and fell in on me.

My foreman, a good man who worried about his casualties, brought in the backhoe to dig me out fast, but they got too close. The scoop grabbed the hardhat and wrenched it off breaking the chinstrap and my neck and twisting my head until some of its horny plates cracked.

At the hospital they fastened wires to bolts drilled into my skull and the company lawyer gave me a check for a quarter million dollars in exchange for a signature on a promise not to sue. I took the money and signed though the thought of suing had never occurred to me.

IV

I was, by my standards, rich. I was out of the hospital, but still bald when I was called to bury my father and while there, "home" in Arkansas, decided to rent the old place, buy the trailer and the feist dog and go live on the rubble of a cabin where I'd spent some of my childhood.

I'd determined, as my head knitted, to resume my studies and ordered all the books I could locate on the overseas Chinese. I wanted to get on with that and maybe go from there to other Asian migrant groups. Then I came across the old shaman's address and decided to see if he was still alive. I wrote a letter, got an answer and a couple weeks later left in my old Jeep truck for the long drive north to talk to him.

Eagle I

The following is the transcript of an interview with Soloman Eagle (hereafter referred to as SE) interviewer's comments are in parenthesis.

SE: I love these trees man. Lord, I was hungry for trees. Grew up in west Texas. Only trees there, I mean wild trees, not pet trees in town. The trees there were all hunkered down and hanging on with both hands. I'm a desert Indian all right, but I sure love these trees. And the water. Water everywhere. That's something for a west Texas boy.

Int.: Ever go into the basin?

SE: Sure. That's the people's home. Went there to learn. Learn best on the home ground, least that's what the man who taught me thought.

(The waitress was at the table.)

Int.: Want any breakfast?

SE: No. Just coffee. Seem to live on coffee and cigarettes anymore.

(Soloman Eagle chain-smoked non-filtered cigarettes. He spoke of himself as old and I knew he was my father's age or older. They'd been in the same war, but he looked younger, an agile middle age. Tall and thin, hisface only lined on the forehead and around the eyes. He wore his hair, salt and pepper, in a crewcut. I mentioned his short hair.)

SE: Those old time boys with their ponytails didn't have worry about gears.

(We walked back from the diner along the highway. Brant, Minnesota was just some stores, a couple of marinas and a few houses strung along the road where it edged the lake.   The town lived on the lake's reputation for walleye and muskie fishing and the summer fishermen this attracted.   Soloman's shop – outboards, small engines, lawn mower and chain saw repair – was in an old gas station, his apartment in back.   The machine shop was like any other, the apartment sparse: two chairs for sitting, two chairs for eating, a table, desk, bookshelves.   A small TV and a big radio and the paraphanalia of a shaman – drums, fans, rattles – hanging on the walls.)

SE: Thoreau was right. You want to get on with living you got to get things out of the way.

Eagle II

(He put the coffee pot on, sat at the table and put an ashtray between us.

SE: My father didn't do nothing but work. Trying to show up folks talking that lazy Indian business I guess. Worked in the oil fields. Worked all day, came home, had supper, went to bed. Had one day off, Sunday, and he'd go find some more work. Never said two words to us kids. Never said much to anybody. Just worked and ate and slept. My folks didn't tell us kids nothing about the people. They thought it was best forgotten. Wasn't popular then. Didn't want to get caught acting like a redskin. I didn't worry about it any ether till the war. Went to Europe, France, Belgium and saw how those people had their history out behind them, lines going back forever. Made me think it'd be nice to have a history too. Made me want to know some. Back in the states I asked around the people that were left, weren't that many even then, and found an old man, a sort of cousin to my father. They said he still knew the old ways. I went to see him and he said he'd tell me. And he did. We'd drive out to the basin and he'd tell me and sent me out to sit and wait for visions. He taught me to dance and to beat the drum and to use the fan

INT: He taught you to be a magician?

SE: I guess that's what you'd call it. Look, the people were all magicians. They had to be to live. They called them Diggers because they dug for roots and ate bugs, considered them contemptible. They had no herds, pueblos. They hunted small game mostly, didn't make war often or very well, but the Anglos couldn't live where they did. Still can't. There's not much in the basin except where they drain the water out of the Colorado to make things grow. The people lived on the earth's breath. They had to listen and understand. They had to hear when the jackrabbits would be thick over here and when the cama roots were ready there and when the pine nuts would be ready there. They had to understand when they should move on so they would get to a new food before the old food ran out. They had to listen to the wind, read the frost and know if a long winter meant the food would be late or if an early thaw would get it ready ahead of time. They had to know every where the earth bled the least trickle of water and where the moist spots sat that could be dug out and give life. A misunderstanding was death. Buffalo couldn't live where they did and the few deer were as scattered and worn-out as the people. They drifted across the earth speaking with her and hearing her words. For a man to live in those days and feed his children was an act of magic.

Eagle III

Int.: What was his name? Your teacher?

SE: Fred, Fred Campbell.

Int.: I mean his real name.

SE: Fred Campbell. Everyone had Anglo names by then.

Int.: You didn't have your own names? In your own language?

SE: Our language was English. The old speech was gone years ago. Don't really know if there was one, there were so few of us. Maybe we just spoke Paiute or Shosone. Who knows? By 1945 you could get the whole tribe around a dinner table and have room for guests.

Int.: You married out of the tribe?

SE: Weren't any girls in the tribe. I married a Miami girl from Oklahoma.

Int.: So you learned your tribe's traditions in English?

SE: Yeah. That and the joke.

Int.: Joke?

SE: Yeah. Fred gave me a notebook taped shut, when he'd finished teaching me. Gave this taped up book and told me to go to vocational school and learn a trade. Told me to get married and get laid a lot and when I heard he was dead to cut the book open. The joke was in the book, but I don't think you'd understand.

Eagle IV

Int.: Why wouldn't I understand?

SE: Look at you, making your notes. Got to have it written, got to get it in a book or under a microscope. Got to skin it and scrape it and hang it on the wall. But there's things you just can't see in a laboratory, things you just have to know.

Int.: Like what?

SE: Like the spirit, man. The spirit inside. Anglos don't really understand that. They look at some guy sitting on the street with no home and no job and, if he isn't missing an arm or leg or something or got a disease, they say he's got bad luck or he's just lazy. Or he's under trained.

That's the Anglo answer to all of life's problems. Give him a pill if he's sick and if he's not, send him back to school. Wouldn't be any homeless if these guys just took data entry. The spirit just doesn't come up in your thinking. If a guys acts to weird, well then he's crazy, his brain is broke and you stick him away with a bunch of other guys with broken brains and give them shots to be good. And counseling. You boys love counseling. Take some vet who can't live very well with some of the shit he pulled when he was a scared shitless kid, can't get through the day without putting enough dope or booze in him to keep his mind off it and you think all he needs is a good talking to. Shit the Anglos love to counsel each other. The only time you boys talk about spirit is in church and then it's not your own. It's got strings on it and old God's jerking it one way and the devil's pulling it another and you got nothing to do but hold on and pray for the best. And it doesn't matter, really, anyway cause you can let your spirit do just any evil it wants to and all you got to do is say sorry about that the last second before you die and nothing you did matters anyway. Do good and it's God's will. Do bad and it's the devil's work. You boys don't do anything for yourselves. Things go to shit, you know, when they set up priests and politicians. When they let others take over. You Anglos have technicians to handle that. Go down to that holy barn once a week and leave your sins behind. Not really your sins anyway, everything's someone else's fault. My boy, you know, was in Viet Nam back in '69. Told me about this guy he knew, was mad about some of the tricks being pulled in the villages, the rape and stuff. Took some pictures with an Instamatic and went to the chaplain. Thought if the chaplain knew, something would be done. The chaplain told him, it can be forgiven. Put it out of your mind.

Eagle V

Int.: You're saying some things can't be forgiven?

SE: Some things can't. Some things can't be forgotten. Shouldn't be. People say these days put this behind you, forget about it. Doesn't matter anymore. You've got to let it go. How can you live without a history? Without memory? Without regrets. If you regret nothing what kind of a monster are you? You've got a society now where anything is all right as long as it turns a profit. Get caught and you pay your fine, maybe do a little time, but nobody's sorry about anything. No one's embarrassed when they get caught. Mortified. I like that word. People used to die from mortification. It's an extinct concept. Anyway, forgiveness is just another way of saying I'm not responsible. Forgiveness is an action taken on you by someone else. Either the person you sinned against ort he society or Jehovah or Yahweh or whatever magical personality you subscribe to. Don't even take the job of correcting your own sins.

Int.: Correct sins? You mean retribution?

SE: Whatever. Whatever you need to do. I don't know if you can really do anything about the sin itself. Remove it or anything. Doesn't matter. The important thing is the man who committed the sin, changing him, making him better. If you are always forgiven, forgotten, bygones are bygones, How can you change? How can you become better?

Eagle VI

Int.: Do you think people can really change themselves?

SE: Sure. Happens anyway, we can't help it. You, you're not the man you were ten years ago. He was a kid. There's echoes and shadows of him in there, but you're someone else now. In another ten years you'll be someone else and when you're my age you'll be someone else again. We change with time. We change our minds. The point is to take some hand in it, take responsibility.

Int.: And when the individual gives over spiritual matters to a priest class society suffers?

SE: Yeah, I guess.

Int.: You think we're taking the easy way out?

SE: Nothing easy about it. The Anglos live hard, man. The way you boys live is good for making money, but it's hard on people. It's hard on kids and old people, hard on people who aren't very sharp, hard on people who aren't hard themselves. You got to be hard to make it and if you're not, you're shit out of luck.

Eagle VII

Int.: You spoke earlier of getting things out of the way. Material things?

SE: Don't sweat the mechanics.

Int.: What?

SE: Don't look for a blueprint.   Nothing's that simple. Crazy Horse did one that worked for him, Buddha did another. Whatever works.   If sitting naked on a hill waiting for God to speak works for you, OK.   Seems kind of stupid to me, but if it works...

Int.: Can we attain, uh, enlightenment in a material world?

SE: Shit man.   Light and dark, black and white. You Anglos got to have everything one way or the other. Light or dark, white or black and nothing in between, but most of the world is shadows man, shades of gray. Isn'hardly anything really just black and white. You guys don't look at the shadows, can't even see them anymore. It's like you look at the top and bottom and miss all that's in between.

(A break here. Soloman had to go to the bathroom. He also refilled our coffee cups.)

SE: OK. Let's say that a man is divided into two parts. There's the thinking part, the intelligence and then there's the spirit. These two things don't get along much. Most of us, we walk around with the two ignoring each other. Anglos mostly go with the intelligence and try to forget about the spirit altogether. Deny it, don't want anything to do with it once in awhile a man gets to where his intelligence and his spirit are working together and become one. That's heaven man. Doesn't happen but once in a while, but often enough that people know it's possible, that's it's a goal to shoot for and have put names to it....enlightenment, nirvana, grace, union with God. Magic man. Those who can reach it now and then are called shamans, mystics, magicians. Those who can maintain it for good are called saints.

Eagle VIII

Int.: All men are islands then, each on his own?

SE: Of course. Of course not.

Int.: What?

SE: We are all unique, isolate, indecipherable. You can't understand another human being no matter how hard you try or how long. My wife doesn't understand me the man says. Nobody understands anyone. And we are all the same, brothers joined at the hip with the same wants, needs. An open book. Both points of view are completely correct.

Int.: There's no right or wrong?

SE: That's not it. I'm saying some things are both at the same time.

Int.: I'm not sure I understand that.

SE: Sometimes understanding doesn't work. You just have to know

Int.: I know I don't understand that.

SE: Neither do I.

Eagle IX

Int.: Did you ever open it? The notebook?

SE: Sure. The day I heard Fred was dead, just like he said. I always did everything just like he told me.

Int.: And?

SE: The joke. The joke was that it was all bullshit. All the stories and dances and songs Fred taught me, the business with the fans and drums and sand writing. All show business. I might as well have learned tap-dancing.

Int.: You mean he made it up?

SE: As far as the people were concerned, yeah. He borrowed most of it from other tribes, the Sioux and Navajo and so on. If the people had any ceremonial stuff if was forgotten before Fred's time. He thought they probably didn't have much, no time for it.

Int.: Why?

SE: Why what?

Int.: Why the games?

SE: Because I needed it. Because I wanted to play Indian. Because I wouldn't have had a chance of getting knowledge without the dramatics.

Int.: But if it's a farce, does it serve any real purpose?

SE: Yes and no.

Int.: What?

SE: No, in itself the ceremony does nothing, summons no one, generates no power. Yes, it serves a purpose. It helps concentration.

Int.: Can you explain that?

SE: The power is in you, in everybody, but you have to get it up, like an erection. Everything you need is here (taps his skull) and in your soul, but you have to find it. If you want to be a witch in the Western tradition, you can't go to a witch store and buy a kit. You have to make it all yourself, the sword and chalice and altar. And you can't just buy a book of book or they have no power. The fact is they have no power anyway. The whole process is only meant to get your attention, make you concentrate and find the real power in yourself. Everyman has the knowledge, but we have big problems. One is you just don't believe it. We have to have the dog and pony show to convince ourselves. And it's hard as hell to clear your head. We've all got worries and hopes and nonsense rattling around in there and we have to cut through all that stuff. You see, all this stuff, meditation and wandering the wilderness seeking God and looking for visions, the fasting and sweat baths and vows of silence and prayer, the drums and fans and rattles, it all serves the same purpose. We're all trying to get to the same place whether you personify it and give it a name like Jehovah or Allah or call it enlightenment or the Tao, it's all the same thing. We just use different slights-of-hand to trick ourselves into finding it.

Eagle X

SE: Are you really interested in knowledge or is this all academic curiosity?

Int: I'm really interested.

SE: Then look back on the tracks you've left. How can you decide where to go next if you don't know where you've been?

The Great American Desert

High Plains

Chris and I were patients in the VA hospital, in the
substance abuse program, both booze hounds drying
out, recovering from withdrawal, gossiping between
groups and sucking on cigarettes as if pulling in the
holy spirit; trying to get a handle on life-without-
drink.

Christopher was an intense, Celtic-dark man glaring
at the world through black-framed spectacles. Until
he drank his way out of it, he'd made his living
feeding cattle. Not his own cattle. He was the hired
hand, wintering on a lonely acreage, huddled in a
little wind-blasted frame house, hauling the wagons
of grain and hay out onto the high plains for the
mindless Hereford and Angus crosses. Dragging the
inevitable dead to a gulch and dumping them,
sacrifice as a by product.

He'd been busted for DUI far too many times to be
allowed a license, so when the night got too thick he
went to the Morton building and fired up farm
machinery, drove to his drink along the shoulder at
ten miles an hour.

A foreigner out in that big empty, nursemaid to five
hundred soulless beefs, forcing his way with the
lumbering, coughing tractor across the blizzard blown

world to the nearest bar, a warm place with warm whiskey to revive the spirit.

When I think of the European presence on the plains I think of Christopher. Half-mad and desperate men who know in their bones that the pacification isn't done yet, that the war continues despite the death of the tribes. Misplaced burghers with the giggling wind forever in their ears feeling fundamentally out of place; still, with their campaigns of plowing and bulldozing and poisoning the countryside, colonizers trying to dominate the land with the issue in doubt. Lake a rapist, the European has bullied the body, but the soul's escaped them. They are the lunatic fringe of the northern Teutonic bourgeoisie, amusingly manic, currying a few feet of lawn amidst the great grassy sea and betting their all on it.

The north slope of the Bible Belt, the church stands tall here and, with its pancake suppers and goodwill dinners, one of two stanchions of social life the other being the town bar, the alternative temple Chris and I chose. The old joke is there are two things to do in this town – go to church or drink. Though the spread of cable and satellite dishes has lessened this, it remains true for those with little love of their own company or a lack of kill times. If you don't drink and it isn't Sunday, if you can't find any work to do and don't care for television, you sit and look at your hands.

Important as the church is, the true passion of the plains is labor. Churches are the second largest temples in prairie towns. Looming over them are the grain elevators.

These people, like the God they worship, are wondrous and terrible. They tend to size: big Nordic types descended from the northern Europeans who slipped south into England years ago and chased the little, dark Britons into the hills while their cousins, having done the same to the Gauls, called themselves Normans and stole Britain from those who stole it first.

Invariably polite, they have little sense of privacy and, with rural guilelessness smile as they chisel relentlessly into your life searching out those little disgraceful nuggets they can share with friends.

Chuckling, they hop out of their truck with the cross hanging from the rearview and the nigger-shooter racked behind the seat, hold out their gun hand for a shake and will build you a barn or a gibbet with equal enthusiasm. Behind their good-natured facades they are whirlpools of conflicting demons. One day they will break their backs and bank accounts welcoming refugees of any color and the next call a Lakota a prairie nigger or spit at Mexican immigrants with the same sincerity, the touching become terrible.

Like with the climate, storms boil up suddenly and the dutiful son with the 4.0 average steals a tank of gas from the Kum and Go and leads police on a high speed chase through two states and seven jurisdictions. The preacher runs away with the lawyer's wife and good dogs sull up and snap. They find a meth lab in the woods behind the Lutheran camp.

They always say, 'but he was such a good boy.'

On the plains our fathers tried to cut America away like a malignancy and graft Europe onto the wounds, but it hasn't been a total success. The grafting persists, force fed chemicals and money and continual transfusions of dwindling ground water, but America remains as well, just under the groomed surface and peeking through the yawning stitch lines. Waiting.

There's too much sky here. It's hard to maintain an ego, so small under heaven and people are tempted to exaggerate themselves, trying to justify themselves with feats of strength, relentless labor, the great lumbering juggernauts of farming. If you can run a hundred thousand dollar short ton of wheeled steel over the landscape all day, you must be worth something and a prairie harvest sounds like an armored assault, the engines of agriculture laying siege to the land.

This is without considering the weather. We live noses to the wind, waiting for the next thing. You're chipping your way out of the winter's last ice storm and look up to see the thunderheads forming. The dry, hot sun beats the ground to dusty steel bleeding topsoil into the breeze, sometimes so much you have to use your headlights downwind, and the rain, when it finally comes, washes you away, seed, stock and grandma, all of it riding the curl down a gully on their way to the Missouri.

We Europeans haven't been here long enough. We haven't learned to drift like the old people. We can't catch the rhythm, but rather squat, build our little squares to wall out all that nothing and crouch inside, peeking out.   We treat our insignificance with arrogance.

The plains don't break you; they wear you away like the paint on your house, until even your memory is gone.   Little graveyards, abandoned amidst somebody's pasturage, have stones still standing, but the wind has whipped away the stories they told.

II

Road Trip

1

With the frontiers gone, until we begin spreading through space, we can only zig zag across the known, bouncing from border to border, touring the purloined goods, carrying our Badlands with us.

The planet will die, one way or another, as will we. The only thing is to go fast and not think about it.

2

The sound of tires on concrete at speed.

I never realize how seriously I listen to it until the song suddenly changes and alarms ring, immediate thoughts of potential disaster: are the tires exploding, the axle disintegrating, the shocks gone cancerous? But it's just a different patch of road, a different mix of asphalt.   Where the season's work was halted by winter, at a state line, where one company's contract ran out and another's began…just a different beat, nothing to worry about until the next sudden rhythm change.

Has anyone, some anthropology major desperate for a new thesis angle, done a study on the similarity between the hypnotic beat of a shaman's drum and the sound of tires on concrete? They both lead to trances.

In my trance I follow the song from northwest Iowa and across South Dakota, voyaging the American steppes. Across it's ridged midsection from which it stretches north to the Arctic and south to Mexico: what they used to call the Great American Desert.

3

My ride is a 1992 Lincoln Town car I bought at the end of its first decade and beginning of its second hundred thousand miles. It has an over-powered eight-cylinder engine that eats fossil fuels prodigiously and shits great clouds of pollution.

The money I spend on this machine would support a family in the Philippines and I love it - American transportation: too much power, speed, comfort, appetite; more than anyone needs of everything; a great, speeding, petro-glutton that was top of the line ten years ago, designed for chasing that relentless dream, or fleeing it; for making time and seeing nothing.

My hermitage, away from nattering children, concerned women, neighbors and relatives and city councils.   Lawns and gas bills and clogged rain gutters. Alone, for Christ's sake, finally.

4

I love driving across the plains at night in a hurtling bubble of light, staring ahead. Look far enough, out there to the tattered edge of your brights, where the beam brittles and shatters against the night, you can see things: fantastic things shining and grotesque, flickering in and out of the eye's field, grinning at you and your disbelief.

These are my visions, fueled on long nights and chain-smoked Luckies and cups of coffee gulped at Casey's as the tank fills; seventy mile an hour visions taken with the radio cranked, but, unlike the visions found by the old people on these same plains, mine reveal nothing. They give no direction or predictions but only dance jerkily at the bitter end of my sight and are gone.

5

Drive long enough, far enough, and suspension of disbelief becomes impossible. You find yourself, eyes burning from headlights and white lines, seeing truth, ready or not. Old illusions no long apply.

Just across the line in Wyoming (Who's line? Why must the line be and why exactly there? What does it separate from what?) the car and I are both nearing empty and I slip in among the semis at a place called Line Stop, advertising food and gas and cold beer, 24/seven. The car fed, I go to the little cafe, order

ham and eggs and the waitress and I collaborate on a
minor lie. The term 'ham and eggs' is a fiction.
What I'm going to eat are really slices from a pig's
ass and unborn chickens. The pig whose ass I'm
eating probably never stepped on grass, but lived its
short life on concrete. Then a truck ride to the killing
factory and the blow, the throat-cutting. The sterile
eggs stillborn to wire bound hens living a life of
pointless births in a universe of sheet tin and piped
grain.

Having these thoughts, while applying hot sauce to
my failed chickens and dipping my toast in them, I
think it's time to pull over for a while, but I won't.
This is exactly the proper state of mind for a
pilgrimage.

6

Once I sought mysteries in the 'wilderness,' skipping
from one patch of woods to another, where they are
allowed to sit in America as carefully groomed as
museum exhibits and nearly as artificial as the
suburbs I ran from, trying to ignore the obvious, this
being that the place I'm seeking is a myth from times
gone by and the real is this thing I'm traveling; a
linear world flanking the interstates that ridge the
continent like a hophead's veins. Pull off at the truck
stop, drive into the diesel air and across the oil stains,
pull in between a Mac and a Kenworthy; cut the
engine and listen to it die, ticking under the hood.
You're home. If there's magic left in the world, it's
here.

7

At a truck stop outside Rapid a trucker tells me I can get laid, if I want some 'Indian poon.' We're in a bar called the Horseshoe drinking ourselves stupid and find we have rooms in the same motel next door.

The trucker says that if I leave the door open, as if for a breeze, the hookers will know you're horny. The cops do too, but they can't prove it. Neither have they figured a way to send undercovers knocking without making it entrapment.

I find his pointless lust disturbing, and touching and holy. He is everybody's nightmare trucker: blasted out of his mind with booze. Red and fat with wild blonde hair and beard, sweating rivers and speaking a wild cursing speech thick with accent and whiskey. He looks barely housebroken and hardly a candidate for trust, the trust to pilot great vehicles with often dangerous cargos at high speeds across the continent, but that's what he does, everyday, year after year with occasional breaks like this one to get drunk, tell tales and leave his motel room door open.

He is, once you talk to him, drink with him and sieve the character out of this drunken parody, just one more nice guy eager to buy drinks and tell his story. I've learned by now that the road has cost him wife and children and he drives long hours to make money he doesn't need anymore. Instead of supporting a family, he spreads it with easy grace among those he meets and befriends, which seems to be anyone who'll take a moment to listen to him and by the time I've declined his party and his offer of cash to, 'drink on me tonight,' and he shuffles off, I know that the hooker who comes through his door will have little work to do and will get more money than they agreed on.

8

I was a sailor for some years and learned that rough, rootless men often carry the spirit, have witnessed more grace in tattooed hulks seemingly born in a nightmare than from the slick suit guys with fifty dollar haircuts. These days sailors are rapidly becoming obsolete as shipping is more and more a matter of automated vessels herded by computer technicians and if there's a second coming on line for America, it will happen on the road among the wandering monks of consumerism wheeling their great cloisters from one warehouse to the next: at some off-ramp motel or a roadside pullover in the shadow of a historical marker commemorating past massacres. The midwifery by a shaved skull ex con, the child cuddled in great arms inked with legends of love and war. The supreme good and direst evil spring side by side from the same flesh beds watered by mirrored passions.

These same lovely men, given the right mix of fear and anger, would slaughter children in a ditch. The difference between saint and serial killer is this: there is no difference.

www.ingramcontent.com/pod-product-compliance
Lightning Source LLC
Chambersburg PA
CBHW052207170626
46812CB00004B/1691